Praise for the Novels of H.J. Ralles

The Keeper Series

"Aimed at young adults, this is ingenious enough to appeal powerfully to adults who wonder how far this entire computer age can go. Ralles knows how to pace her story - the action moves in sharp chase-and-destroy scenes as Commanders hunt down the dangerous young boy. The characters are memorable, particularly the very human 101. And that ending . . . -is brilliant. A compelling read from exciting beginning to just as exciting ending." –**The Book Reader**

"*Keeper of the Kingdom* is a must read for children interested in computers and computer games. From the first page to the last there is no relief from the suspense and tension. H.J. Ralles has captivated anyone with a fascination for computer games, and has found a way to connect computer-literate children to reading." –*JoAn Martin, Review of Texas Books*

"Kids will be drawn into this timely sci-fi adventure about a boy who mysteriously becomes a character in his own computer game. The intriguing plot and growing suspense will hold their attention all the way through to the book's provocative ending." –**Carol Dengle, *Dallas Public Library***

"This zoom-paced sci-fi adventure, set in the kingdom of Zaul, is a literary version of every kid's dream of a computer game. Keeper of the Kingdom may be touted for youngsters from 9 to 13, but I'll bet you my Spiderman ring that it will be a "sleeper" for adults as well." –**Johanna M. Brewer, *Plano Star Courier***

"As in any good video game the PG-rated action is unrelenting, and the good guys never give up. *Keeper of the Kingdom* could be made easily into an adequate Nickelodeon-style kids' movie." –*VOYA*

"H.J. Ralles continues to offer readers a fascinating affiliation between computers and books. Her two 'Keeper' stories are wonderful reading experiences." –*The Baytown Sun*

"H.J. Ralles spins a wonderful Science Fiction tales aimed at younger readers, but has also created something that is quite enjoyable for book lovers of all ages." –**Conan Tigard, *ReadingReview.com***

"Ralles knows how to turn out a first-rate story. And, how to make coming-of-age as suspenseful as nature makes it every day." –**Lisa DuMond, *SFSite***

"*Keeper of the Empire* is a fun read, with action that grips you from the start. Excellent for middle school and reluctant readers; enjoyable and suspenseful." –**Christie Gibrich, Roanoake Public Library, Roanoke, Texas**

The Darok Series

"*Darok 9* is an exciting post-apocalyptic story about the Earth's last survivors, barely enduring on the harsh surface of the moon . . . An enjoyable and recommended novel for science fiction enthusiasts."*–The Midwest Book Review*

"*Darok 9* has the excitement of a computer game, put into a book, that parents and teachers will love to see in the hands of their children." **–Linda Wills, *Rockwall County News***

"*Darok 9* is another wonderful science fiction book for young adults by H.J. Ralles, author of Keeper of the Kingdom. Filled with nonstop action and suspense, it tells the story of a young scientist, Hank Havard, and his quest to keep his big discovery out of enemy hands. The language in this book is clean, as it was in Keeper of the Kingdom, something I found refreshing. Also, the message that violence doesn't pay is strong. The characters are believable, and the plot is solid. Darok 9 is a can't-put-it-down, go-away-and-let-me-read science fiction thriller, sure to please any reader of any age!" **–Jo Rogers, *Myshelf .com***

"From the explosive opening chapter, the pace of Darok 9 never falters . . . Ralles holds us to the end in her tension-filled suspense. We read on to see what surprising events her interesting characters initiate. The scientific jargon and technology does not interfere with the action-filled story which any person can follow even if less versed in the science fiction aspects." **–JoAn Martin, *Review of Texas Books***

"H.J. Ralles is the author and creator of this science fiction book for kids. However, Darok 9 certainly can hold its own in the adult world as well. This very entertaining book is hard to put down. Once you start reading it you just want to know how it will end. Filled with action and surprises around every bend this book keeps your attention." **–Kelly Hoffman, *Slacker's Sci-Fi Source***

"In the near future, Earth has been ravaged by ecological and military disaster. The few who survived have gone to our Moon, eking out an existence in domed towns called Daroks (Domed AtmospheRic Orbital Kommunities). Our plucky protagonist is a scientist researching ways to reduce the need for water by humans. Little does he know that treachery and betrayal lay all about him. An attack on the remote lab by the Fourth Quadrant sets him running from more than just falling masonry . . the double-crosses and double-double-crosses should be engaging for a young adult. **–*Space Frontier Foundation, Moon Book of the Month Club***

KEEPER

of the

ISLAND

Keeper of the Island

By

H.J. Ralles

Top Publications, Ltd.
Dallas, Texas

Keeper of the Island

A Top Publications Paperback

First Edition
12221 Merit Drive, Suite 950
Dallas, Texas 75251

ISBN#: 1-929976-39-9
Library of Congress Control Number 2007922322

The characters and events in this novel are fictional and created out of the imagination of the author. Certain real locations and institutions are mentioned, but the characters and events depicted are entirely fictional.

Printed in the United States of America

For

Joe, Brenda, Polly, Robert and Pam; Morley, Debbie, Paige,
Bert and Elaine—
who don't let me get away with anything!

"In a writer there must always be two people—the writer and
the critic." Leo Tolstoy

Acknowledgments

I want to thank all of those people who have nurtured me, and my writing, throughout the whole Keeper series—from the thrashing about of ideas to the complicated process of publication.

Foremost I am indebted to my family for putting up with me and my writing moods. Thanks to my friends and critics in my writing groups, to whom this book is dedicated—you guys certainly gave me plenty to think about every session. A big thank you to my editor, Brenda Quinn, who helps my stories grow up into books.

Thanks also to the children who won my website competitions or gave me inspiration for some of the characters in my novels: Jesper Mount for Jesper of the Mount in Keeper of the Empire, Varak Baronian and Sarven Orak for their namesakes in Keeper of the Colony, and to Darian Thomas and Sara Brown for Cap'n Persivius Scarr and Skimmy McFinn in Keeper of the Island.

And finally, it was my good fortune to have my first manuscript accepted by Top Publications in 2000. Thank you to Bill Manchee for his support of my work over the last six years.

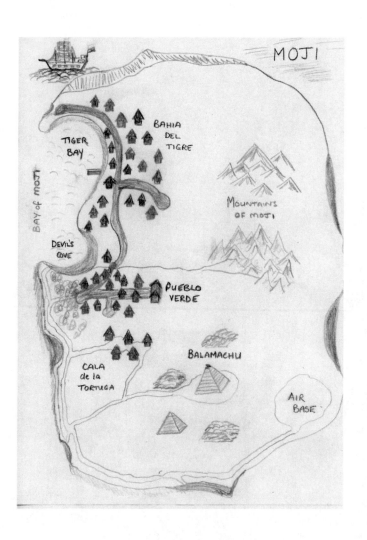

Chapter 1

"**U**gh! I think I'm going to be sick!"

Matt lay on the floor clutching his stomach. His head was spinning, the smell of salt and tar was overpowering, and he seemed to be swaying. To make matters worse, it was so dark that he could hardly see. And what was that splashing sound?

"Gotta get some fresh air," he gasped, clambering to his knees. But every direction he crawled, he bumped his head on something hard. He stretched out his hand and felt around. It seemed he was in some kind of container with curved sides. Was that a bench seat he was touching?

His stomach continued to churn and his ears rang. Perhaps he would feel better if he stood up. But as he lifted his head it hit some kind of tarpaulin above. He was trapped! He broke out in a hot sweat. "What is this place?"

He ran his hand across the tarp to where it met with the curved wall and managed to squeeze his fingers between the two. A shard of light filtered through the tiny gap and he could just feel a thin cord attached from the tarp to something protruding from the other side of the wall. He shoved his hand harder through the gap, fumbling until he had unwrapped the cord and loosened the tarp.

Brilliant sunlight burst into his confined space. Matt drew back, and then after his eyes had adjusted to the light, forced his head through the hole he had created.

A crazy mass of blue and white surf rolled and splashed below, making his head spin even more. "No way!" he grumbled. "I can't be at sea!"

He strained his neck to look up. Towering above him appeared to be the rear of an old sailing ship. He could see a row of leaded windowpanes, and what did that blue cursive writing on the wood say? He couldn't quite read it. He undid a second cord, loosened the tarp further, and forced his head back until he could just make out the letters. "*Dreamseeker*," he read.

A small black and white flag flapped high atop a pole, occasionally unfurling as the wind dropped. Was that a skull and crossbones he just saw? He shook his head. "Don't be ridiculous, Matt!" he shouted. "You're seeing things!" His imagination really was working overtime.

His stomach churned and another wave of nausea passed over him He lowered himself back under the tarp and sat on the floor with his head bent forward, listening to the creaking of the ship and the splashing of the sea. Now the curved walls made sense. He was sitting in a small boat suspended above the ocean at the stern of what seemed to be an old 17th century galleon. "Crazy computer game!" he growled. "I can't believe I chose to do another level of *Keeper of the Kingdom.* I must have been an idiot."

"Heave-Ho!" came a loud voice from above. And then again, "Heave-Ho!"

Suddenly the little boat jerked. The creaking grew louder and louder. One end of the boat rose . . . then the other. Matt's heart pounded as he was thrown violently back and forth. He grabbed onto one of the benches to stop himself from tumbling across the floor. What was happening? Something hard hit his foot before sliding past him and coming to rest under the seat at the bow of the little boat. Matt groveled on the floor and just caught a glimpse of his black laptop as he was thrown into the middle of the boat once again. His laptop! That was great news! His heart raced with excitement.

All of a sudden the boat stopped tipping and the tarpaulin was thrown back. Staring down at him was the puffy, angry face of a middle-aged man with wild jet-black hair and a thick matted beard.

"Well, I'll be! What 'ave we 'ere, me mateys?" the man snarled, his lips curling upward into a sinister smile. "I do believe it's a young 'un! I thought I 'eard a kid shout. Where's Skimmy McFinn?"

"I'm 'ere, Cap'n Scarr, sir."

A second face peered over the railing. It was an older teenage boy with dark skin and a golden ring in each ear. His tightly curled black hair escaped from beneath a red scarf tied around his head.

Matt started to stand up. "I think I'm going to be sick," he announced.

The captain instantly stepped back. "McFinn and Rogers, pull the young 'un out of the jolly boat and lock 'im in the brig!" he snarled.

"Aye, aye, Cap'n, sir," said Skimmy.

Matt heard a huge cheer, which sounded as if a hundred men were gathered on the deck. "The brig! The brig! Put 'im in the brig!" they chanted.

"The . . . b . . . b . . . brig?" Matt stammered. His stomach knotted. The accents of these men, the headscarves, the earrings—not to mention the black flag with the skull and crossbones on it—they all seemed to point to one thing. "You're not pirates, are you?"

Captain Scarr leaned over the edge of the boat and adjusted his tricorn hat. "Aye, me lad, that we are." His breath reeked of liquor. "I'm Cap'n Persivius Scarr and you're aboard me ship." He laughed loudly. "Thought you wouldn't be caught, did ye? We've 'ad plenty of young 'uns like you wanting to go to sea, and they all think that 'iding in a jolly boat is clever. Obvious place, don't you think? We'll teach you a lesson you'll not forget. To the brig with you! That's what we do with stowaways."

"Stowaways? But I'm not a st . . . st . . . stowaway," stammered Matt. "I was just looking around."

"Just looking around?" Cap'n Scarr tipped back his head and roared. "Never 'eard that excuse before. Enough of this nonsense! Billy Rogers, get 'im out of the jolly boat, now!"

Matt stared at the men who were gathered around the boat as he was hauled out. They seemed to be a strange mixture of people. Some of them were dressed in jeans and brightly colored T-shirts and could have been from his hometown, while others were dressed in pirate clothes. And they were all applauding and laughing at him.

Skimmy McFinn and Billy Rogers—a huge hairy pirate with a belly that rolled over his belt—dragged him along the wooden deck by his arms. Matt managed to lift his head to see tall white sails billowing in the wind. He wasn't sure whether his churning stomach was from seasickness or from fear. Was he really onboard a pirate ship?

"Please, I'm gonna be sick. I need a bathroom," mumbled Matt. But both men ignored him and dragged him along the deck until they reached two slatted trap doors near the bow.

Rogers let go of Matt's arm and heaved open the doors. He let them fall against the deck, causing an enormous crash. "Down there with ye!" he growled, shoving him toward the opening.

Wooden steps descended a long way into darkness. Matt shakily clambered down the steps and watched as the doors above banged shut, enclosing him in an eerie tomb. He sat on the floor and listened to the jangling of metal. Through the slats he could just see Skimmy McFinn chaining the doors together. His heart sank. Escape was unlikely.

Within a few minutes Matt's eyes had adjusted to the near darkness and he could just make out his tiny prison.

Fragments of light found their way in through the gaps between the planks of wood that formed the walls of the ship.

He shivered in the damp cold. He wondered how he would be treated. Would they bring him food or a blanket? The only good news was that he knew his laptop was in the jolly boat. But how could he retrieve it?

Suddenly there seemed to be some sort of commotion on the deck. He could hear men shouting and running above him. Then there were the sounds of grating metal and moving chains. The floor seemed to judder—in fact, even the sides of the ship seemed to judder. Was the anchor being lowered? He listened hard but couldn't make out what the pirates were saying.

Then Matt heard voices that didn't seem to be coming from onboard the galleon. He crawled around the confined space struggling to squint through the gaps in the wood. Finally he found a small hole and, with one eye pressed against it, he caught a glimpse of the jolly boat. Matt gasped. Skimmy McFinn and Billy Rogers were rowing away from the ship, and taking his computer with them! Then they were gone from his vision. Would they notice his computer under the front bench? Would they give it to Captain Scarr? And would the jolly boat return to the galleon? He had so many questions and no one to answer them.

Matt felt utterly miserable. He was a prisoner onboard a pirate ship and neither Targon nor Varl were anywhere to be seen. Every level of his computer game had been harder. Why had he expected Level 5 to be any different?

* * * * *

Varl watched the mosquito land on his elbow. He slapped his arm hard. "Gotcha!" he snarled. He scratched his arms, then his legs and ankles. The mosquitoes were eating him alive! Sitting under this tree in the tall grass was a mistake. Just where had Matt's computer game landed him this time?

He looked around him, careful to stay hidden in the grass. What might he face this time? It wasn't long ago that Gulden Guards dragged him off in the Colony of Javeer!

The air felt thick, and judging by the lush vegetation and the constant cawing of strange birds he guessed that he was somewhere in the tropics. Was that the sea he could hear? His heart quickened. He hoped that he wasn't stranded on some deserted island. Immediately he envisioned himself with a long beard, surviving on coconuts, and going mad from years of loneliness. That would be awful! Enough dreaming and complaining! It was time to stand up and find the boys.

The branches rustled loudly. Varl looked up expecting to see an exotic bird or a monkey. Instead, beneath the mass of foliage, he could see dangling legs and a pair of familiar brown shoes.

"Targon? Is that you?" asked Varl, getting to his feet.

The branches rustled again and then parted. Targon

peered down at him, his thin face framed by straggly blond hair. "Varl? Thank goodness *you're* here!"

"Zang it, my boy! What are you doing up there?"

"How do I know? Matt's stupid computer game, I suppose. Just help me get down, please!"

"I don't know what I can do from here," said Varl, feeling helpless. "I think you've got to crawl along to the trunk. The branches below you are fairly close together. You should be able to climb down."

"It looks a long way to the ground," said Targon, inching along the branch he was straddling.

"Try not to look down . . . oh, and try not to fall."

"Funny," said Targon, his voice quaking. "I suppose you'll catch me if I do."

"You'd flatten me!" Varl laughed.

"True, but at least *I'd* survive."

Varl laughed again. "Okay, you're nearly there. Just another few inches. Great!"

"Whew!" said Targon, wrapping his arms around the trunk. "That feels a bit better. At least I'm holding onto something that doesn't sway!"

"Now shift your left leg round to where the branch below sticks out," said Varl. "Easy does it. Now lower yourself again. Good." Suddenly Varl heard an almighty crack. "Watch out! The branch you're standing on is about to—" There was a loud snap.

"Ahhhhh!" screamed Targon as he fell, knocking Varl to the ground. The branch landed on top of them both, followed by a shower of leaves and splintered bark.

Varl groaned. Now his old bones would ache even more.

Targon rolled off and began shaking him. "Varl! Varl! Are you okay?"

"Yes, I think so," said Varl, sitting up. "I'll just be a bit sore tomorrow."

Targon laughed. "You were right when you said I'd flatten you!"

"Okay, my boy, enough with the jokes. Help me up."

Varl winced as Targon pulled him to his feet.

"Are you alright?"

"I'll be fine once I get moving again."

"Have you any idea where we are?" asked Targon.

"Not a clue. But everything I've seen and heard so far would suggest we are near to the coast somewhere in the tropics. I can even smell the sea from here. Could you see anything from up in the tree?"

Targon shook his head. "I was too scared to do anything other than keep my balance and think about getting down."

"Pity."

"So which way do you think we should go?"

Varl was already walking. "Let's head for the sea. If we're lucky we might just find Matt on the way."

"Wait, Varl!" said Targon, grabbing hold of his arm. He lowered his voice. "Is that someone singing?"

Varl listened for a few seconds. Targon was right. How sharp of the boy to have picked out that sound from the background of bird songs. He wondered if his hearing was deteriorating as well as his sight.

"Should we hide behind the tree?" questioned Targon.

Varl nodded. He hobbled back to the tree and painfully lowered himself in the grass. Targon crouched beside him, peeking occasionally around the trunk.

"Careful," whispered Varl. "We can't take any chances until we know where we are, and what or who we're dealing with."

"Don't worry. They won't see me."

"Get down! They're getting close," said Varl. "And keep still."

"But the mosquitoes—"

"Shh!"

The grass rustled. The words of the song became audible. Varl listened intently. The tune was catchy and sounded like an old sea shanty.

"Yo-ho, Yo-ho, Yo-ho, Yo-ho
We're just back from sea, me mateys
The ships got no wind in 'er sails
The ol' skull an' crossbones still flyin' up 'igh
Black and white against the blue sky
So ye landlubbers better beware
Ye landlubbers better beware."

The singing stopped and chatter took over. Now Varl could make out two very different male voices: the singer's was deep and raspy while the other was higher pitched and probably younger. *And* they were getting louder. Varl's heart pounded. He'd been in this situation so many times before in Matt's computer game. What would their enemy be like this time? He shuddered when he thought of the Vorgs. Maybe they'd meet up with a friend and not an enemy.

Now the voices were clear and very loud. These people—whoever they were—were standing on the other side of the tree! Thank goodness Targon had finally stopped fidgeting!

"Well, I ain't never seen a boy so green before! He's definitely *not* got sea legs. I thought he was going to puke all over Cap'n Scarr!"

"Aye, Billy. But the cap'n wouldn't 'ave stood for that. The boy's lucky. As 'tis, the cap'n made us throw 'im in the brig."

Varl gulped as he watched a mosquito land on his leg. He didn't dare move. It would just have to suck his blood.

"So what d' ye reckon the cap'n 'll do with him now?"

"Beats me. The cap'n can't let 'im come with us tonight— 'e'd 'ave a mutiny on 'is 'ands! Way too dangerous. 'e'll disembark 'im with the rest of the visitors."

Now Varl's knee joints began to ache. He tried hard not move, but it was no good—he had to shift his position.

"Shh! Did ye 'ear somethin', Skimmy?" said the deep raspy voice.

"Nah, Billy. There's no one out 'ere but the birds."

"You sure? Best we lose the pirate accent like Scarr told us. Don't want nobody thinking that we're real pirates."

"Yeah, I forgot. Scarr would kill us. I just get into such a habit of talking like that!"

"What was I saying, Skimmy?"

"The boy. We were talking about the boy. Scarr will surely interrogate him. The kid's strange, don't you think? Strange accent—and he's blond! He's not one of the kids from this island, for sure. I can't believe he denied being a stowaway."

Targon tapped Varl's arm. His eyes were wide with excitement as he mouthed, "It's Matt! It's Matt!"

Varl clamped his hand over Targon's mouth and frowned at him.

"He may have just been looking round the ship," continued Skimmy. "Like he said he was doing. You know, interested like."

"Nah. I reckon the boy's a spy. Sent by the government to catch Cap'n Scarr."

"Well, if ye ask me, he don't know nought about pirates and he don't know nought about our ship."

"You don't say! Skimmy, that much was obvious. But that's a good thing—'cause the boy won't go sticking his nose in where it don't belong. Now let's go and do what we came here to do. This bag is mighty heavy."

The voices faded. Varl kept his hand over Targon's mouth until it was clear that the two men had gone. He sighed deeply with relief. "That was close—you nearly gave us away!"

"But did you hear what they said?" asked Targon. "They've got Matt! Matt's onboard a pirate ship!"

"Hold on for just a minute," said Varl. "We don't know that for sure. It could be any boy."

"How many boys do you think are around here who seem strange, have blond hair, don't speak like the locals and are onboard a pirate ship claiming to be looking around?"

"Not many, that's true. But it doesn't necessarily mean it's Matt, either."

Targon shrugged. "I'd be willing to bet on it."

"Well the words *island* and *pirates* certainly got my attention. That means no way to leave here except by boat, and if we're dealing with pirates we've got serious problems."

"Pirates?" laughed Targon. "Aren't they just in stories? Matt gave me a book about pirates to help with my reading. Besides, I thought pirates were around hundreds of years ago. Matt's game is supposed to take place on Earth in 2540 AD."

Varl shook his head. "There have been pirates in just about every age and there'll be pirates in the future—going after different types of booty with different kinds of vessels. They're real enough. Most are bloodthirsty, murderous thieves—and it looks like we're going to have to deal with them, my boy."

"We are?"

"We're changing our plans."

"What plans?"

"We were heading to the sea—but it's no longer the best plan," said Varl, struggling to his feet. "If it *is* Matt they were talking about, they're our only connection to him right now. We need to follow those pirates and find out as much as we can about them before we try any kind of rescue."

"Well, let's hurry up about it—before we lose them!" said Targon.

Chapter 2

The chains jangled. Matt looked hopefully at the wooden trap doors above him. They began to open. He shielded his eyes as sunlight flooded into the tiny room. Were the pirates releasing him or just checking on him?

"Out with yer!" bellowed a throaty voice.

Quickly he made his way up the rickety steps.

A gaunt bald man with a patch over his left eye yanked him off the top step and onto the deck. "Cap'n Scarr wants to see yer."

"He does?" Matt's heart pounded. What would Scarr do with him? He'd heard about pirates making their victims walk the plank—and much worse. He drew in a deep breath. "Is he going to let me go?"

"That'll be for 'im to decide. Now get walkin'."

"Where to?" asked Matt.

"The cap'n's cabin, of course."

"And where's that?"

"In the stern. Just walk."

After his confinement, Matt tried to take in every detail on his walk along the deck. Some of the pirates were lowering the sails and the three tall masts rose into an expanse of brilliant blue sky.

Matt paused and looked over the side. The ship was

anchored in a bay ringed by a white sand beach. He had a sudden urge to jump overboard and swim ashore. He was a pretty good swimmer but could he make it that far?

"Keep walkin'!" yelled the pirate. "Or I just might throw ye to the sharks! The waters round Moji are infested with 'em."

Matt gulped. Jumping overboard wasn't a good idea after all. Swimming in shark-infested waters would have to be his last option. He looked longingly at the beach and the lush hills in the distance. Freedom seemed so close.

Suddenly he heard sounds in the water. Was that an engine spluttering? How could that be? This was the 17th century! He stared down over the railing. Men, women and children dressed in jeans and T-shirts were leaving the *Dreamseeker* and climbing aboard a small motorboat. They certainly weren't pirates!

And what was that anchored in the distance? A huge modern cruise ship with a radar tower! But how was that possible when he was in the 17th century standing on an old galleon? It was as if two time periods were colliding right in front of his eyes.

"What's going on?" demanded Matt. "Who are those people getting into that motorboat? And what's that huge cruise ship doing here?"

The pirate shoved him in the back. "Keep movin'! Ye can ask Cap'n Scarr when ye get to 'is cabin."

Matt suddenly felt a surge of renewed courage. Something didn't seem right about any of this. He thought back to when Skimmy McFinn and Billy Rogers had hauled him out of the jolly boat. Everyone was shouting and he'd been seasick at the time, but hadn't he noticed a strange mixture of people standing on the deck? They hadn't all looked like pirates. Now he was sure of it.

They reached the captain's cabin and the pirate kicked the door. "Cap'n Scarr, sir. It's 'awkeye and I 'ave the boy as yer requested."

"Bring 'im in!" bellowed Scarr.

Matt tumbled forward as Hawkeye pushed him through the doorway. He tripped on an uneven floorboard and fell flat on his face.

"Get up!" said Scarr.

Matt felt embarrassed at his pathetic entry into the room. He stood up proudly and took several steps forward until he was standing directly in front of Captain Persivius Scarr. The grotesque man smelled as if he'd been working with pigs. He was sitting at a long dining table in front of his cabin windows, stuffing bread and soup into his already puffy cheeks. Matt grimaced as the soup spluttered out of the corners of the captain's mouth and dribbled onto his matted beard.

Matt summoned up the nerve to speak forcefully. "Captain Scarr, sir, I demand that you let me go!"

Persivius Scarr wiped his arm across his mouth in one long motion, brushed his wild hair out of his beady eyes and snarled, "You *demand?*" He shoved his bowl angrily to one side, jumped to his feet and thumped his hands down on the table. His bulging face turned beet red, his lips puckered and his little eyes seemed to spring from their sockets. He leaned across the table, spitting food over Matt as he bellowed, "And just who are *you* to demand anythin'?"

Matt cowered, his courage waning. "I'm Matt. Matt Hammond, sir," he said in a quiet voice. "And I want to know why you're holding me prisoner."

"Because *you* were 'iding on my ship!" said Scarr, still bent across the table, staring at him. "Who sent you, Matt 'ammond?"

"Sent me?"

"To spy on me and me crew."

"Spy? I'm not a spy. No one sent me. I was just looking round your galleon and I fell asleep in your jolly boat."

"Galleon? This is no galleon! *This,* boy, is a three-masted square-rigger." Scarr's eyes narrowed and he looked at Matt suspiciously. "She carries up to two 'undred men an' twenty-four cannon, an' she's a beauty, ain't she?"

"Two hundred men?" said Matt. "There's really two hundred men onboard this ship?"

"There used to be." Scarr smiled, showing a set of wildly crooked teeth. "You don't know nought about pirates, do you, boy?"

Matt shook his head. "No, not much."

"Ahh, the sea air," the captain said, turning to point to his open cabin window. "There ain't nothin' like a fresh sea breeze. It seems you don't know nought about ships either."

"I've never been onboard a gal . . . square-rigger before."

"And you 'adn't 'eard about paying to come onboard me ship?"

"Paying?" said Matt. "What do you mean by paying?"

"Me and me crew, we sail from port to port givin' tours around the *Dreamseeker*—educatin' local folk about pirate life and old sailin' vessels. If you'd paid like everyone else who came onboard we would 'ave treated you nice like." His face once again took on a more serious expression. His eyes narrowed and he added, "But I don't like 'avin' unwanted visitors 'board me ship!"

Matt frowned. *Pirates giving tours?* "So you're not really pirates then, you're actors?"

"Actors? Certainly not!" snapped Scarr. "We're pirates, all right." He paused as if he'd thought better of his comment and smiled a crooked smile. "But not as you're thinkin' of pirates. An' let me tell ye, boy, we're still the kind of pirates you wouldn't want to cross."

Matt shook his head. Were they pirates or not? "So you give tours around the *Dreamseeker*," he said. "Is that why I saw all of those people getting into boats just now?"

"Ah! You saw them, did you?" Scarr walked around to Matt's side of the table and leaned over him. Matt recoiled at the man's bad breath. "We 'ad to make an example of you, boy—throwin' you in the brig 'n all." Scarr glared at him. "I don't want the local kids thinkin' they can just come aboard when they want, messin' with me ship." He fingered Matt's blond hair and then tugged at it sharply.

"Ouch!" Matt pulled away.

"But you're not one of the local kids, are you? They're all dark skinned and 'ave deep brown eyes, *and* their 'air is jet black—not blond and spiky on top. And just look at your bright blue eyes. And then there's your clothing. . . just what do you think you look like?"

Matt's heart raced. How could he get out of this one? He looked down at his garments. He was totally out of place, still dressed in the bright red baggy pants and top from Horando Javeer's gold mines in Level 4 of his game. "Er . . . no, I'm not one of the local kids," was all he could think to say.

"So what exactly are you doin' 'ere?" questioned Scarr.

"I'm on vacation and I'm staying with a friend for a few weeks."

Scarr ran his fingers along the gold brocade that edged his long blue jacket and then folded his arms across his chest. He stared Matt squarely in the eyes.

"On the other side of Moji," said Matt as an afterthought. Perhaps that would make his story sound more convincing.

"The other side of Moji, eh?" Scarr's voice hardened ruthlessly. He perched on the edge of the table. "Did you see anything else while you were 'appenin' to look over the side of me ship?"

Matt frowned. Did he see anything else? What did

Scarr mean? He thought for a minute and replied, "There was a cruise ship anchored in the bay."

Scarr seemed to relax a little. "Okay, boy. We'll let you ashore. But I'm warnin' you—I don't want to see your face back on me ship without a ticket! If I do, you won't be in me brig for thirty minutes—you'll be locked in me brig for thirty days or more! Do I make meself clear?"

Matt nodded. "Yes, Captain Scarr. Perfectly clear."

"Good. Now be off with you! You'll just make the last boat ashore if you 'urry. Make your way down through Gun deck to Orlop deck and you can board from there. We've added a special boardin' ramp for our modern-day guests near the bow."

Matt scooted to the door quickly.

"And Matt 'ammond," said the captain, following after him.

"Yes, sir?" said Matt, turning toward him, one hand firmly on the wooden doorknob.

Scarr's mouth twisted into a sinister grin. "If I should find out that you've been lyin' to me, boy, me men will be out lookin' for you. And I guarantee," he shouted, "there'll be no place on Moji or any other island that you can 'ide from me!" A thin chill hung on the edge of his words.

Matt swallowed hard. He managed to mumble, "Yes, sir," as he backed quickly out of the room. Whew! He looked up at the sky and drew in a deep breath. He was free to go!

Hawkeye was still standing outside the captain's cabin. He grabbed Matt by his collar, spun him around, and warned, "I'll be watching you, boy! They don't call William 'awkins 'awkeye for nothin'! I may only 'ave one eye, but I can see better 'an those with two."

Matt shook himself free. As he straightened his shirt and walked away he heard Scarr whisper to Hawkeye, "I don't want no more meddlin' kids onboard. It's too risky—we'll 'ave the authorities pokin' around."

Matt headed across Main deck in search of steps down to the lower decks. As he passed by the crew, many stopped what they were doing, cheered "Yo-ho-ho!" and laughed at him. Matt was sure of one thing—he had been their amusement for the day. But why did he still feel so terrified? These men weren't really pirates. But Scarr had hinted at something sinister, and his words to Hawkeye seemed to confirm that. Something besides tourism was happening onboard the *Dreamseeker*. Something that Scarr was worried Matt had seen.

A wave of relief washed over Matt when he saw the steps down to Gun deck. He charged towards the open hatch.

"Careful ye don't trip on the coamin'," shouted a pirate carrying a heavy sack over his shoulder.

"The coaming?"

"The rim round the edge of the 'atch," he explained. "It stops the water runnin' off the top deck and gettin' down below during a storm."

"Thanks," muttered Matt, somewhat surprised by the first friendly conversation since he'd arrived onboard.

Down on Gun deck there were no pirates in sight.

Twelve polished cannons were lined up along each side of the narrow hull, tidy piles of cannonballs in between them. Matt walked along the deck, stopping to study some of the cannons and touching the long barrels. It was obvious that they hadn't been used in years. Now, where were the steps down to Orlop deck? He couldn't wait to get on that little boat and head for shore.

Matt froze. Head for shore? What was he thinking? He couldn't get off the *Dreamseeker* until he'd retrieved his laptop. And that meant he had to wait for Skimmy McFinn and Billy Rogers to return in the jolly boat.

Matt sat down between two cannons, his back against the ship's hull. His heart pounded and a lump rose in his throat. He had no choice but to stay onboard. But where could he hide? *Not here*, he thought, looking around the spartan Gun deck. But if he didn't find a hiding place fast, Captain Persivius Scarr would lock him in the brig. And Matt didn't want to return there anytime soon.

Chapter 3

Targon stared at the fork in the trail. "Which way do you think the pirates went?" he asked Varl.

"Look at the ground. See how the grass on the right is freshly trampled?"

Targon nodded. Obvious, wasn't it? Why hadn't he noticed that? For an elderly man who often complained about his deteriorating eyesight, Varl was still pretty astute. Targon grabbed his hair, which was sticking to his neck and bothering him in the heat, and pulled it into a bunch. "Okay, we're going to the right," he said, forging ahead.

The mosquitoes got worse as they headed into the denser vegetation, and he angrily swatted them away. The trees were taller and close together, allowing little light to penetrate between them, and now ferns and vines replaced the grass underfoot. Even the bird sounds had changed, from the loud coarse caw of the colorful parrot-like birds to the twittering of smaller ones. He stopped to scratch his legs from time to time, telling himself that he was giving Varl a chance to catch up. Truth was, the mosquitoes were driving him mad. Red welts dotted his legs and arms, and scratching them only made the itching worse.

Suddenly they came to a clearing. In front of them stood a huge stone pyramid. Targon had never seen anything like it. He looked up in awe, squinting in the brilliant sun. The structure was so tall it seemed to disappear into the blue.

"Wow! What *is* this thing?" he asked Varl.

"Well, judging by the crumbling stones, the elaborate carvings and the vegetation growing on the sides, I'd say it's some kind of temple or burial tomb left by an ancient civilization."

"How tall do you reckon it is?"

Varl shielded his eyes and looked up. "At least one hundred feet."

Targon walked round the outside wall. He fingered the huge stones. Moss grew between the layers and in some places the stones were completely covered by thick grass. Occasionally writing was carved into the sides. He traced the letters but they were unlike anything he had just learned to read. He wished he could understand what was written. There were also other shapes in the rock—complex patterns and carvings that seemed to resemble faces.

"They're called stucco friezes," said Varl, coming up behind him. "I read about such things when we were back in Zaul. Many ancient civilizations were known for their elaborate art."

Targon continued round the next corner. On this side of the pyramid, steps rose as high as he could see.

"Well, that's it! No doorways or tunnels to get inside this thing, and I didn't see any paths into the rain forest anywhere around the base, so I guess we've reached a dead end," said Targon. "Unless you've got any other brilliant tracking techniques for finding pirates."

Varl laughed. "If you're following someone and they disappear, it's not a dead end."

Just as Varl finished talking, Targon heard voices above. "It's them! It's the two pirates," he whispered. "They must have climbed this thing."

"Go back round the corner and stay flat against the side of the pyramid," ordered Varl. "Quickly!"

Targon's heart pounded so hard that it seemed to reverberate throughout his whole body. He kept still and pressed himself close to the wall. Would the pirates be able to see him, even though they were coming down the other side? He heard chunks of rock and loose gravel fall as the pirates made their way down the crumbling steps, their banter getting louder as they neared the bottom.

"Are ye alright, Skimmy?"

"What ye askin' me that for, Billy? You're the one with the big belly. I'm surprised ye can see where yer puttin' yer feet."

Billy roared. "I gotta feel for this kinda thing. Besides, we've done it lots lately—trekkin' back an' forth from ship to shore 'idin' the booty. It's the 'eat that gets me, not the steps. This island must be the stickiest place on Earth."

"Yer sweatin' buckets, fer sure. Don't collapse on me now, will ye!"

"Nah. Don't ye worry, Skimmy. We're nearly at the bottom. Goin' up was much 'arder with the 'eavy load we 'ad."

"Yeah, it was a lot of booty today."

Targon heard a thud close by. One of them must have jumped the last few steps. He caught his breath.

"There, Skimmy, flat ground again—but I'm not a landlubber, fer sure."

"You saying landlubber made me realize that we forgot to lose the accent again," said Skimmy. "It's hard to remember."

Billy laughed. "Don't worry—Scarr's just paranoid. Look around! There's no one to hear us. This is the rain forest, for crying out loud! Even the tourists don't come this far inland."

"Yeah, I guess you're right. We'd better get back to the *Dreamseeker*. Cap'n Scarr has a fit if everyone isn't on deck to raise the sails."

Targon waited a few minutes for the voices to fade, then exhaled heavily. He slumped down on the grass. Hiding from those goons twice in one day was more than he could take. "I think they've gone," he said.

Varl patted him on the shoulder. "See, I said it wasn't a dead end."

"Now we know the name of the ship that Matt's on!"

"Indeed—the *Dreamseeker*. And we also know she's a sailing ship. That's a valuable piece of information. So what are you waiting for? Get up and get yourself ready," said Varl.

"Ready for what?"

"To climb."

Targon chewed his lower lip. "You're joking, right? Why would you want to go up there?"

"There are ancient burial chambers to see," said Varl without hesitation.

Targon felt annoyed. "You want to waste time going up to see burial chambers?"

"And more importantly, the pirate booty," said Varl, winking. "Let's see what they've been stealing."

"Haven't you taken a look at those steps?"

Varl fingered the stone in front of him. "They're crumbling a little, but they're pretty wide."

"But can you make it down again?"

Varl laughed. "I'm not going—you are! There's no way I'll make it up the steps with my arthritis!"

Targon's heart was racing once again. "So you want *me* to go on my own?"

"Do you have a better idea? Right now this is the only lead we've got, my boy. We need to know what they're hiding up there and you're the only one who can find out."

Targon thought quickly. "We could follow the pirates back to their ship instead," he suggested.

"We'd never keep up with them now that they've got rid of their heavy load. Besides, we've got time. The ship will be there for the next few hours. They'll have to wait for the tide, and then it'll take time to hoist anchor and raise the sails."

"But we might be able to get onboard before she

sails," said Targon.

Varl shook his head. "The only way we'd be able to get onboard without being seen is in the dark. If the ship is still there tonight we'll see if it's possible."

Targon groaned. "Okay, you win. I guess I'm climbing this monstrosity. Good job I've not got a fear of heights like Matt."

Varl smiled. "Even Matt would climb this *monstrosity*, as you call it, if it meant beating his computer game."

"You're right, he would," said Targon, starting the climb. "But this is not going to be easy." He placed each foot carefully and used his hands to steady himself. His legs shook a little as the steps narrowed and he got higher. He hadn't gone far when he paused and looked down at Varl.

"How are you doing?' Varl shouted.

"Fine," said Targon.

"Any sign of a ship?"

"The tops of the trees are in the way, but I think I can see the sea through them. I've never been to the sea."

"Well, you'll get a chance later."

"I can't see any ships."

"See anything else?" asked Varl.

"There are two people walking away from us along the trail. I guess it's the pirates. But they don't look like pirates. They're wearing jeans, T-shirts and baseball caps."

"They didn't talk like pirates all the time, either," said Varl. "What did you expect them to wear in these modern times—scarves, eye patches and gold earrings? Keep going," ordered Varl.

Targon turned back around to face the pyramid and carried on up. The steps deteriorated as he climbed higher, obviously more exposed to the wind and the rain. His feet slipped occasionally, but he comforted himself in the knowledge that if a fat pirate like Billy Rogers could make the climb, it ought to be easy for a teenager.

Finally, he reached a plateau just below the pinnacle. Right in front of him was a narrow tunnel with steps leading down inside. This had to be where the pirates had hidden their booty! He looked down to tell Varl what he had found and saw the same two people walking back towards the pyramid along the trail. Why were they coming back? If those really were the pirates, he and Varl were in serious trouble!

Targon opened his mouth to shout a warning to Varl but then stopped. A shout would give them both away. So instead he waved madly, hoping the pirates wouldn't look up and see him. But Varl just waved back with a smile, not recognizing Targon's distress signal.

Targon watched in horror as the two men entered the clearing.

"Hey, you! What are you doing here?" one of them shouted, his voice raspy and familiar. Now there was no doubt and it was too late. The two pirates had entered the clearing and were running toward Varl.

Targon's stomach was in knots. He crouched down in the entrance to the tunnel, trying to stay hidden and yet observe what was happening below.

"Who were you waving to?" the man with the raspy voice yelled.

Varl didn't answer.

"Is someone up there?" the same man questioned.

Varl still didn't answer.

Targon stifled a scream as they drew guns from their pockets.

"Put your hands up!" the man snapped.

Varl quickly raised his hands above his head.

Targon's heart skipped a beat as he watched the scene below. What was happening now? Varl was climbing the pyramid! The pirates were on his heels, forcing him up the steps and one of them was poking his pistol in Varl's back. But how would Varl make the climb with his bad knees?

He had to find somewhere to hide before they got to the top! He looked around. The path that had once circled the top of the pyramid was crumbling in so many places, so that wasn't an option. Without further thought, Targon entered the tunnel and started down the winding stone steps. He had no idea what he would find at the bottom, but whatever was down there was better than being taken prisoner by the pirates. Then what use would he be to either Varl or Matt?

* * * * *

Matt squatted between the cannons on Gun deck

trying to work out where he could hide until Skimmy McFinn and Billy Rogers returned in the jolly boat. His choices were limited. If he went back up to the Main deck he'd be recognized instantly, so he had no option but to go down to Orlop deck. But the bow, where people were boarding the boat ashore, was the last place he wanted to end up. He needed to be at the stern of the ship where the jolly boat would be suspended when McFinn and Rogers brought it back.

Matt looked around Gun deck. There seemed to be three sets of stairs: one at each end and the set he'd come down in the middle. Carefully he made his way aft, ducking for a few seconds between each cannon and checking over his shoulder. He peered down through the open hatch. Steps? This was no more than a ladder. He grabbed the handrail. There didn't seem to be anyone below, but then he couldn't see much except a small area at the base of the ladder. He *could* hear voices but they seemed distant. Going down was risky, especially as he would have to go backwards.

He descended as quickly as he was able until his feet touched the deck. The ceiling was low and his hair brushed the beam above. Suddenly someone grabbed his shoulder! He jumped, totally caught by surprise. He turned to find himself staring directly at a pirate's hairy chest erupting through an open shirt.

"Oy, boy! What yer doin' down 'ere?" The pirate's protruding front teeth were a deep shade of yellow.

Matt's knees shook. The pirate was hunched over

between the beams. His thick curly hair matched the rug on his chest. "Er, Captain Scarr sent me to Orlop deck to board the boat to Moji. But I can't seem to find it." Now he was done for. Scarr would send him back to the brig for sure.

"That's because yer come down at the wrong end of the ship—yer in the tiller room. I'm Bart and I be the tillerman. I steer the ship."

"Oh," said Matt, quite taken aback by yet another friendly pirate. "I guess that's an important job."

The tillerman smiled proudly and pointed up at the long pole overhead. "Indeed it is. This is the 'ead of the tiller an' it changes the angle of the rudder when the helm is turned."

"Cool." Matt reached up to touch the pole, trying to appear interested. Perhaps he might get away with this after all. "So how do I get to the boarding ramp?" he asked casually.

"Just keep walkin'—through the surgeon's cockpit, the powder room and then the sail room. Yer'll see it. Best ye 'urry, boy—the last boat's soon to go. Now I gotta go and 'elp swab the deck or Cap'n Scarr will 'ave me 'ide. I can't wait to stand up straight for a few hours!"

"Thanks for your help," said Matt, almost tripping over the tillerman's feet in his eagerness to depart. "I'm sure I'll be okay now."

"Just don't go down to the 'old and yer'll find yer way fine."

Matt watched the tillerman climb the ladder back up

to Gun deck and then stumbled through the doorway to the adjoining room. He had to find a hiding place!

The ceiling in this room was even lower. He was 5'6" and even he had to hunch over. He had to be in the surgeon's cockpit. The floor was painted red and a variety of tools were laid out in a tray on a low wooden table.

"Gross!" said Matt, shuddering as he picked up a curve-handled knife and a sharp tool that looked like one of his dad's screwdrivers. "I can't believe that they used to operate on pirates with these things!" *Operate? More like cut open*, he thought, as he put the tools down and looked around for somewhere to hide.

The room was sparse—no boxes, barrels, or furniture that might provide some camouflage. He was just contemplating moving on to the sail room when he noticed a long low cupboard built into the curvature of the hull. Matt opened one of the doors to find that although the cupboard wasn't very deep, he could lie down with his legs stretched out. It would be cramped, but it was the ideal hiding place for a few hours while he waited for Billy and Skimmy to return.

Matt squeezed inside and pulled the door closed. He tried in vain to get comfortable with his back against the wooden timbers of the hull. It was hot and smelly in the confined space, but at least he felt safe, since the tourists had left for the day and Orlop deck seemed empty of pirates.

As he lay in the darkness, his eyelids became heavy

and he wondered if he dared nap for a few hours. He was just beginning to doze off when something furry brushed past his face and scampered down his leg. Matt froze. Rats! There were rats onboard!

Chapter 4

Targon pressed his hands against the cold stone walls to steady himself as he descended into the pyramid. He counted four steps and then a wider step on a turn, another four and then another turn. And so the pattern continued. The light from the entrance faded slowly as he went deeper, until he found himself searching for the edge of the steps in total darkness.

His determination faltered when it dawned on him that with just one slip he could fall! He mumbled to himself, "Why am I doing this?" His voice seemed to echo eerily. He breathed deeply. There was no going back—not if he wanted to avoid capture by the pirates and perhaps even rescue Varl. He had to continue.

Slowly he felt for the next step and then the next. Would he ever reach the bottom? He counted twenty more. Finally he shuffled forward again—but the step wasn't there. He bent over and felt the ground. Loose sand and gravel fell through his fingers. At last! He *had* reached the bottom. Now could he find somewhere to hide in the darkness? He inched carefully forward, feeling his way with his left hand against the cold wall.

Suddenly there was a bang followed by a bright flash, as if lightning had just struck. He jumped with the shock. A woman appeared before him, shrouded in pink light.

She wore a long white robe and a gleaming golden tiara.

Targon blinked twice. His mind must be playing tricks on him in the darkness! He shook his head and blinked again, but she was still there, her long dark hair blowing around her face. Heart thumping and knees wobbling, Targon reached out to touch her. Was this yet another hologram? But his hand touched a solid figure. He gasped. She smiled and nodded her head in a knowing way.

"I am the Gate Keeper of Balamachu, the spirit of Queen Elena." Her silky voice was soothing and yet carried a unique force.

How could this be a spirit when he could touch her? "Keeper, did . . . did you say Keeper?" Targon squeaked. Surely this was no coincidence. Was he already playing Level 5 of Matt's *Keeper of the Kingdom* game?

She nodded. "Who are you who dares to enter the tomb of King Bakana Kimile, first leader of the Kayapuche tribe?"

"Targon . . . I'm . . . I'm Targon."

"Please state your business with the king."

Targon was floored. If this was a tomb, wasn't the king already dead? "My business with the king?" he repeated.

"What is it that you require of him?"

"A place to hide," said Targon, not knowing what else to say.

"What is the password for entrance into the burial chamber?" Elena turned and pointed at the black wrought iron gate behind her.

"Password?" said Targon, looking around in the half-light. "I don't know any password."

She placed her palms together as if she were praying and bowed her head. "Then I'm sorry, but I cannot be of help to you. In order for me to open the gate you must provide the password."

Targon opened his mouth to plead for her help, but she was gone, and he was once again in darkness. His heart sank. Now what? At least, thanks to the temporary light, he had a rough idea of his surroundings. While the spirit had been talking he had taken note of where the shadows fell on either side of the gate. As long as the pirates didn't have a torch or flashlight, he just might be able to stay out of sight. It was all he could hope to do. He shuffled over to the gate and felt his way along the wall. He was just positioning himself when he heard voices above.

"Get down there, old man!"

"But I can't see where I'm stepping, and my legs are very shaky after that climb," pleaded Varl.

"Enough of your moaning. Skimmy and I have things to do and we've no time to be dealing with you."

"But I really don't think I can—"

"Get going!"

Suddenly Targon heard tumbling rocks followed by a gut-wrenching scream. "Ahh!" The sound echoed and echoed. "Ahh! Ahh!"

The scream shot through Targon's heart. He was

sure that it was Varl who had screamed. The old man must have fallen. There was an eerie silence followed by low painful groaning. Targon didn't know what to do. He couldn't even see if Varl was badly injured.

"Now look what you've done, Billy! You shouldn't have pushed him!"

"And what else was I supposed to do? We couldn't leave him up there."

They'd pushed him? Targon was horrified. He held his breath. Varl had been right about pirates—they were bloodthirsty, murderous thieves. *Murderous*? The word sent chills down his spine. What if Varl died from the fall before he could help him?

Suddenly a pink light illuminated the tomb and the spirit reappeared. Targon pressed his back hard against the wall trying to remain hidden.

"I am the Gate Keeper of Balamachu, the spirit of Queen Elena. Who are you who dares to enter the tomb of King Bakana Kimile, first leader of the Kayapuche tribe?"

"I'm Skimmy McFinn."

"I'm Billy Rogers."

"Please state your business with the king," said the spirit.

"We wish to make an offering to King Bakana," said Skimmy.

"And to save you time asking more questions, the password's Dreamseeker," snapped Billy.

Dreamseeker, thought Targon. *Got to remember that.*

"You may enter the tomb," said the spirit.

Targon watched in amazement as the spirit of Queen Elena waved her arms in a figure eight above her head. The heavy black gate swung open and torches magically lit the tomb beyond. The warm orange glow that filtered through the gate illuminated Varl, sprawled across the floor at the base of the steps. He wasn't moving! Had they killed him?

Tears welled in Targon's eyes and his stomach tightened, but he dared not move. Skimmy and Billy were armed. Skimmy and Billy? Those names were too innocent for these brutal murderers. Anger welled inside him. He would think of them as McFinn and Rogers. Those names would be permanently etched in his mind. He'd bring them down for what they'd done to Varl, if it was the last thing he did!

"Will that be all?" the spirit of Queen Elena asked.

"Yes, that's all," said Skimmy McFinn.

"Now leave us alone," Billy Rogers growled.

"Do not remove anything from the tomb or there will be consequences," said the spirit. Then she disappeared, leaving the two pirates bent over Varl.

"Did you kill him?" asked McFinn.

Billy Rogers kicked Varl. Varl groaned.

"There's your answer," Rogers said with little emotion. "He's still alive, for all the good that'll do him."

Targon swallowed hard. At least Varl was alive.

"What do you mean?" asked McFinn. "We can't just leave him here to die."

"Well, he's not coming back to the ship with us. Captain Scarr would keelhaul us for sure. Hey, the old man can be our offering to King Bakana!"

"I thought the booty was our offering every time we came," said McFinn.

Rogers laughed loudly. "Don't be so dumb. I was joking—you know, human sacrifices an' all that! Besides, there's no real offering to King Bakana. That's all just part of the things we have to say to get past Queen Elena and get the gate opened."

McFinn wound his black curls tightly around his forefinger. "I just don't like the thought of leaving someone to die. He's bleeding badly, too."

"You've gotta think of yourself first," snapped Rogers. "The old man'll die if his time is up, and he'll live if it isn't. I don't see no one else down here, so let's go into the tomb and get rid of the booty in your pockets that we forgot to dump the first time around."

"Then let's get out of here," said McFinn.

"And don't use the pirate accent on the way back," said Rogers. "We don't want any other nosy tourists following us."

Targon drew in a deep breath. Could Varl hold on until the pirates had gone? *Patience*, he told himself. *Just a few minutes more.* He finally heard the gate close.

Rogers stepped over Varl and began climbing the steps. McFinn paused. "Sorry, old man. It was an accident," he muttered. "Billy didn't mean to push you so hard."

"You're too soft, Skimmy," said Rogers, continuing up.

The lights from the chamber flickered and slowly died, and once again Targon was in darkness. He waited for a few minutes to be sure that the pirates had gone, and then crawled across the floor to his friend.

He gently shook Varl's lifeless form. "Varl, are you okay? Can you talk to me?"

Varl didn't answer. Targon felt sick. He shook Varl harder. But there was still no response.

* * * * *

"Zang it!" Matt whispered. Something was tickling his ankle—probably those darn rats again. *I can't stand it any longer. I've just gotta get out of here.* His legs were cramped from lying in the cupboard for hours. The last boat ashore had surely gone by now. But had McFinn and Rogers returned in the jolly boat? Dare he come out of his hiding place?

Carefully he opened the door—but only an inch. Low light seeped through the crack from a small electric lantern suspended in the middle of the room. Thank goodness the ship had been modernized for the tourists! He shifted his position to look at his watch. It was eight o'clock and, he hoped, dark outside.

He opened the cupboard wider and listened for a few seconds. No voices—just the creaking of the ship. Gently he eased himself out of his hiding place and scrambled to his feet. The next few minutes would be crucial. He knew that he had to stay to the rear of the *Dreamseeker*, but that meant climbing the ladder from the tiller room up to Gun deck and then up the steps to the Main deck—and all without being seen!

Matt tiptoed to the doorway and peered through. There was no sign of Bart the tillerman so he dived for the ladder, scrambling up as fast as he could. Just before the top, he paused and peered cautiously across Gun deck. He looked through the gunports and was very pleased to see a dark sky. There wasn't a soul in sight, but above he heard music. Perhaps everyone socialized and ate dinner on the upper decks.

Matt retraced his path, hiding between the cannons until he reached the steps mid-ship. He paused at the bottom. Would anyone be standing directly at the top? Would there be any place to hide at the top?

He'd just have to hope that the distraction of the festivities would be enough cover. He had to retrieve his laptop from the jolly boat and that meant he had to go all the way across Main deck, up to Quarterdeck and up again to Poop deck!

He crept up the steps and very slowly peered over the top at his surroundings. At least forty men were sat in a large circle around the base of the main mast. Their seats were tea chests, barrels and boxes, and several of the pirates were up high, sitting with their legs hanging through the rigging while joining in with the singing. It was difficult to make out the faces in the glow of the lamps, but Matt didn't think Captain Scarr was amongst them.

It was a cloudy night with a half-moon, which meant there would be few shadows. Three pirates sat with their backs to him directly in front of the steps up to Quarterdeck. As long as he didn't make a noise this could be to his advantage.

The shanty finished. "I'm gettin' me some more grog," said one of the three pirates. He got up to refill his drink. Matt ducked. Was that the end of the entertainment? He hoped not, or he'd have to get back down to Orlop deck in a hurry. The fiddler started to play another sea shanty and the pirate returned to his seat. Matt sighed with relief.

Out of the shadows one of the pirates got to his feet and began to dance. The others clapped and cheered, tapping out the rhythms on various objects while tipping back their drinks. The dancer was young and nimble. He wove in and out of the barrels and makeshift seats, his feet moving quickly. Light from the lanterns on deck highlighted his face as he turned in circles. Matt gasped. It was Skimmy McFinn! Excitement surged through him. If McFinn was back from Moji, so was the jolly boat! He'd make his move now while everyone was captivated by McFinn's talented footwork.

As Matt clambered through the hatch, he tripped over the coaming, landing flat on his face directly behind the three pirates. His heart beat wildly. Had they heard him? But the music and the sound of chatter and singing covered his fall.

Skimmy McFinn reached the edge of the circle and

the pirates all looked left to follow his movements. Matt scrambled to his feet and hid behind the barrels of grog. He waited patiently until McFinn was once again on the other side of the deck and all heads were turned in the dancer's direction. Then he snuck up the steps.

Now he had to cross the rest of the Quarterdeck to get to Poop deck at the rear of the ship—and there were few places he could stop and take cover on the way. His worst fear was that the pirates sitting on the main rigging would see movement down below. His heart was racing. It was now or never.

He crept low from shadow to shadow, and between the few cannons on the Quarterdeck until he reached the mizzenmast, the huge pole that supported the aft sails. Matt drew in several deep breaths. The stairs to Poop deck were within view but so was Captain Scarr's cabin. He was just about to make a dive for the stairs when he heard a creaking noise. The door of Scarr's cabin began to open.

Oh no! He slid round to the other side of the mizzenmast, praying that his dark clothing would conceal him in the dim light.

Matt instantly recognized the voices—it was Scarr and Hawkeye. He listened intently, trying to block out the sound of the music from farther down the deck.

"So, it's agreed, we'll take 'er tonight," said Scarr. "Assemble a shore crew for tomorrow. You'll need four men this time. There'll be a lot of booty to stash after this 'un. And after what 'appened yesterday, I want you to go ashore with 'em—and I want you to go at dusk."

"But that can be risky in a jolly boat with no lights, Cap'n."

"It's 'ow it 'as to be. We've been gettin' too confident. We've got to be more careful."

"Aye, Cap'n."

"Check things out, 'awkeye. An' make sure you all change out of your pirate costumes before you go ashore. We don't want no nosy locals makin' any connections with this ship."

"Aye, Cap'n. I've got four good men. Skimmy McFinn and Billy Rogers can say too much at times, but they 'ave proved themselves trustworthy an' they follow me orders without question."

"Who else?"

"I'll be takin' James Elrod as coxswain an' Conan O'Malley—'e's a good shot, should we 'ave trouble."

"Good choice, 'awkeye."

"An' what of the ol' man, Cap'n?"

"Ahh! Rogers did well. If the old man is still alive when you get there tomorrow, leave 'im to die. Word'll soon get out and then we won't 'ave no more meddlin' tourists at Balamachu."

"Aye, Cap'n. It'll be done as ye say."

"Now back to tonight's business, 'awkeye."

"We're ready for the raid, Cap'n. Twenty men, two teams of ten."

"Good. We go in two hours—and no mistakes tonight. It's big pickin's."

"Are ye expectin' trouble, Cap'n?"

"Nah. Just check the big guns before they go—and I don't mean the cannon!" He laughed.

"Aye, sir."

Matt heard the cabin door shut and Hawkeye's heavy footsteps across the deck. He moved slowly round the pole so that he wouldn't be seen as Hawkeye passed by.

Matt realized his knees were shaking. Something was going down tonight and again tomorrow, and he didn't like the sound of either event. And on top of all that, the mention of an old man being left to die sent shivers down his spine. Were they were talking about Varl? Persivius Scarr–actor, pirate or whatever–was an evil man.

Matt needed his laptop urgently. He had a feeling that when he opened up Level 5 of his *Keeper of the Kingdom* game, he'd have a better idea about what Scarr was doing onboard the *Dreamseeker*.

Chapter 5

Targon tried to wipe away the flood of tears. Was Varl dead? He pressed his head against Varl's chest, but he couldn't hear a heartbeat. Surely the old man wouldn't die on him. He *couldn't* die on him! Targon needed him!

No, Varl was too strong. He'd endured so much at the hands of the Cybergons and on his many adventures with Matt. Targon tried to compose himself. He pressed two fingers against the old man's neck. Yes, he could feel a faint pulse! If only Matt were here to help—he'd know what to do. But Matt wasn't here. It was up to him, Targon, the boy from Zaul, to save the old man.

"Varl! Wake up!" he shouted, shaking him again. But it was so dark he couldn't tell if Varl had moved. "Light . . . I need light."

Targon knew only one way to get light in the tomb. He crawled along the floor until he reached the gate. "Spirit of the tomb. Are you there?" he shouted, getting to his feet. His voice echoed faintly. "Spirit of the tomb! Please help me and my friend!"

Nothing happened. He rattled the gate but it was firmly shut. How could he get the spirit to appear and light the tomb? "Spirit of Queen . . ." What was her name? He racked his brains. Queen Elena, that was it! And she was

Gate Keeper of Bala-something. He stood and thought for a moment more. "Balamachu!" He was sure of it. He tried again. "Gate Keeper of Balamachu, spirit of Queen Elena. Are you there?"

And suddenly Elena was next to him, shrouded in bright pink light.

"Yes!" he shouted, imitating Matt.

"I am the Gate Keeper of Balamachu, the spirit of Queen Elena. Who are you who dares to enter the tomb of King Bakana Kimile, first leader of the Kayapuche tribe?"

"It's Targon. I wish to make an offering to King Bakana. The password is Dreamseeker," he said quickly.

The spirit of Queen Elena waved her arms in a figure eight above her head. The heavy black gate swung open and the torches magically lit. Targon's jaw dropped and his eyes widened as he saw what lay in the tomb beyond. "Zang it! There's a fortune here!" he declared, totally entranced by the piles of dazzling jewelry.

"Do not remove anything from the tomb or there will be consequences," said the spirit of Queen Elena.

As if in a trance, he walked slowly through the open gate and into the tomb. He couldn't stop himself. On one side were boxes stacked to the ceiling, overflowing with diamond necklaces, gold bracelets and sparkling gemstones of every color, while on the other side were piles of clear plastic bags filled with currency from many different countries. Targon had never seen so much money and jewelry. He picked up some of the beautiful necklaces, turning them every which way under the torches so that the gems caught the light and sparkled. *So this is booty,* he thought.

At the back of the tomb were eighteen huge shiny metal crates. Targon knelt and examined them. Each was padlocked and marked DANGER CGP in bright red. CGP? The letters meant nothing to him. Perhaps Varl would know. Varl! Suddenly the booty didn't seem to matter. How could he have been so preoccupied when his friend lay dying?

He turned and ran back through the gate toward the foot of the stairs. Targon shrieked in horror. Where was Varl? His heart thumped madly as he ran to the place where Varl had lain. Turning in circles he felt hot and then cold. Varl was gone!

* * * * *

Matt waited for the clouds to cover the moon and darken the sky. Quickly he climbed the creaky steps to the Poop deck, praying that Scarr, in his cabin below, wouldn't hear him. He leaned over the stern of the ship under the lantern. It wasn't a long way down to the jolly boat—just a few feet, in fact—but it wouldn't be easy to get to. He sighed. At least the boat was there!

He thought back to when the pirates first hauled up the jolly boat and dragged him out. Hauling up the boat was not going to be an option—he didn't have the strength or the know-how to do it on his own. Besides, the noise would instantly bring the whole pirate crew up on Poop deck.

As he peered over the stern he knew what he had to do. Matt climbed up on the railing and looked down. For a moment he felt dizzy, but he was slowly conquering his fear of heights and this would surely be the ultimate test. Below was the jolly boat, covered by a tarp that was tightly stretched across the top and tied at intervals with thin cord.

He drew in a deep breath, closed his eyes and leaped off the side, bouncing a little before coming to rest on the tarp. His heart pounded as he lay there trying to catch his breath. Before he was swept into his *Keeper of the Kingdom* game never in a million years would he have jumped off the back of a ship!

Now he had to get *in* the jolly boat. He loosened the cord and pulled back a small section of tarp, then slithered onto the front seat of the boat. He reached underneath for his computer. His heart sank when he couldn't feel anything but a coil of rope. Surely the pirates hadn't found it!

Matt lay on the floor and pushed himself under the seat, stretching his hand into the bow. This time his fingertips touched something metallic wedged under the front. *Yes! It was still there!* He freed his computer and hugged it firmly. Now Level 5 of his game could really begin.

Matt couldn't wait a minute more. He opened the lid,

powered up his laptop, and tapped his fingers on the case while the game loaded. Excitement and anticipation raced through him. What would be in store for him this time?

A pirate jig played as a picture of a full moon over stormy seas replaced the initial blue screen. He lowered the volume.

"Welcome, me hearties, to *Keeper of the Kingdom*," announced a husky voice. "Ye be enterin' Level 5, *Keeper of the Island*."

Matt couldn't help but laugh. The pirate accent gave him no doubt that he was supposed to be onboard the *Dreamseeker*.

"Ye are about to navigate the Island of Moji on expert difficulty. Do ye wish to continue with yer most daring challenge yet, or are ye a landlubber? Press *yes* if ye have the courage to risk the cat o' nine tails."

Matt didn't hesitate as he pressed *yes.* "Let's see what my challenge is this time," he muttered.

A three-masted square-rigger appeared on the screen, battling the raging seas.

"It's the *Dreamseeker*," he whispered. "Now for the rhyme."

In Level 5 as in Level 2
Deactivate the Keepers so you can rule
Onboard *Dreamseeker* not all is well
There's discontent and trouble to quell
Find the mutineers to help your game

Use the islanders to do the same
Below Orlop deck you will find
This pirate ship's not of its kind.

He leaned back against the bench seat. The rhyme seemed complicated, but then the rhymes always did to begin with. He read it a second time. Mutineers? All the pirates had seemed very happy to him. In fact, the mood onboard was positively festive. And islanders? Did that mean he had to get off the ship at some point? Deep down he hoped that was the case. He'd already had enough of life onboard the *Dreamseeker*, and longed to explore the white sand beaches of Moji. But for now he knew that he would have to stay. "Below Orlop deck you will find this pirate ship's not of its kind," he read out loud. At least it was a starting point. That meant he had to get back down to Orlop deck while it was still dark.

Chapter 6

Targon stared at the floor of the chamber in disbelief. He'd left Varl alone for only five minutes—how could he have disappeared in such a short time?

"Varl!" he shouted. "Varl, are you there?"

There was no response, just the usual faint echo. Targon walked over to where he had hidden in the shadows earlier and checked that Varl wasn't slumped against one of the walls. The burial chamber was a small enclosure consisting only of the open area by the stairs and the chamber itself where the booty was stored. As far as he could see there was only one way in or out of Balamachu.

The gate to the tomb banged shut, and the lights dimmed. There was nothing left that he could do, especially in the dark. With a sudden burst of energy, Targon leaped up the steps. The old man had been unconscious when he'd left him, but just in case by some miracle he'd come to and made it up the steps, it was worth checking for him at the top.

The bright sun hit Targon as he emerged from the tomb. Judging by its position in the sky he guessed it was late afternoon. He stood at the top of the pyramid, turning in every direction, and then walked around the top peering over the edge, but there was no sign of Varl. In the distance he could just make out McFinn and Rogers heading back along the trail at a fast pace. He sat down, totally bewildered and unsure of what he should do next.

After fifteen minutes of sitting in the sun, Targon realized that he was burning, but he still hadn't got a plan. He had stayed in the tomb hoping for a miracle, but now he realized that a miracle was not going to happen and he needed to do something to find his friend.

He was desperately thirsty. First he had to find water. Then, he'd search the area around the base of Balamachu.

He descended the pyramid feeling more optimistic. At least he finally had a plan. However, he had no idea where to find water and he didn't remember passing any streams earlier in the day.

He was about to walk back along the trail when he heard rustling in the trees. Just as he turned, a slim girl in her early teens emerged from the dense foliage. He stepped sideways to avoid her.

"Oh!" she said, obviously startled to see him. Her dark cheeks flushed.

Targon raised his hands to show her he meant no harm. "I'm sorry," he apologized. "I didn't mean to scare you."

She looked down, avoiding his gaze, and her long black silky hair fell forward. "No, it's okay, really." She twisted her hair into a thick bunch, wrapped it around her hand and then let it spring free. "I was in my own little world and I just didn't see you. No harm done."

"I don't suppose you know where there's a stream, do you? I've been out in this heat for a long time and I'm desperate for a drink."

She didn't answer his question but stared at him for a few seconds and said, "You're not from around here, are you?"

Targon shook his head, looked down at his clothing and then at her sleeveless dress and bare legs. "It's a bit hot for long pants, socks and shoes, I guess," he replied.

Her face split into a wide grin. "That too," she said, laughing. "But I was thinking more of your blond hair and pale skin. It gives you away as a tourist."

"A tourist?" repeated Targon. "Oh, yes. That's it—I'm a tourist." He wasn't about to argue with her. How could he expect her to believe a story about being in Matt's wild computer game?

She stepped closer. "So, what's your name and where are you from?"

"I'm Targon and I'm from the Kingdom of Zaul," he said without thinking.

Her dark brown eyes widened. "I've never heard of it."

"Er—it's a very small place, so you probably wouldn't have," Targon said quickly, hoping to avoid questions about where exactly Zaul was. He didn't really know himself!

"Where are *you* from?" he asked, hoping she'd tell him where he was.

She frowned. "This island—Moji—of course!"

"Yes, Moji—of course," repeated Targon. "But what town, I mean?"

"Oh, I see." She offered him a forgiving smile. "It's a village, actually—a little place called Pueblo Verde, which is on the coast. It's only about ten minutes' walk from here. And my name is Gabriela Kimile, by the way."

Targon suddenly felt awkward. Shaking her hand seemed too formal so he shoved his hands in his pockets, bowed his head and said, "Nice to meet you, Gabriela."

"So, Targon, what are you doing here and where's everyone else in your group?"

"My group?"

"Are you with Happy Holidays or Adventure Vacations? They're the usual tours who come to Moji, but they don't usually visit Balamachu."

"They don't?"

"No. This is a private site. It's actually part of my ancestors' ancient burial grounds, and the tribe has kept ownership all these years. I guess your tour guide must have got special permission from my father."

"Oh," said Targon, wondering how he could answer that without causing more problems for himself. Gabriela was chatty and almost too friendly. At this rate she'd be taking him to find the tour guide!

"I can take you to Bahia Del Tigre to find your tour guide for you, if you like," she said, as if reading his mind.

"Bahia Del Tigre?"

"Tiger Bay," she translated. "That's where all the cruise ships come in."

Targon smiled. "Actually, I'm not really with a tour. I'm on vacation with my friends Matt and Varl. We were exploring the area on our own and just stumbled on Balamachu—but then I lost them both."

Her thick dark eyebrows raised inquiringly. "Lost them? That's not good. If you tell me how you got separated perhaps I can help you find them again."

"That'd be great," said Targon. "But I've searched around here already and I really need to get some water from somewhere."

"Oh, sorry, I forgot you said you were thirsty. We'll go to my village—it's the nearest place anyway. I'll get you something to eat and you can tell me about your friends."

Finally—this was the kind of help he needed. As he followed Gabriela back into the dense undergrowth, he turned and glanced back at Balamachu—hoping that he might see Varl standing at the top waving at him. But, no, that's where the good news ended.

* * * * *

Matt had a problem. How was he going to climb up the rope from the jolly boat to the Poop deck? Fortunately, it was only a few feet, but in his eagerness to retrieve his computer he'd been focused on jumping down. Not once had he thought how he would get back up again—and carry a computer.

There was a chill in the night air and Matt suddenly realized he didn't have his jacket. Zang it! His jacket would have been very helpful right about now. He'd often used it to carry his laptop. But at the end of Level 4 he'd been wearing the regulation red linen shirt and drawstring pants from HJG mines—and that was what he was still wearing.

He pulled at the baggy clothes and sighed. Climbing up the rope with the laptop would be impossible in this gear. What could he do?

"Zang it!" he said out loud. "That's it! Sarven's backpack!" At the end of Level 4 he'd pulled his laptop out of Sarven's green backpack in order to enter the final commands. He remembered Varl and Targon had crowded over him, and he'd put his computer down on the top flap of the backpack.

Matt put his computer on the floor of the jolly boat and felt under the front seat. Nothing! He moved to the middle bench seat and finally the rear bench seat. Just as he was about to give up, his fingers touched canvas. The coarse fabric was unmistakable. "Yes!" he exclaimed, reaching all the way under to retrieve it. What luck!

Matt put his computer carefully inside the backpack, slung the pack over his shoulders and scrambled back onto the tarp. As he began the climb he remembered Mr. Daniels coaching him up the ropes in school. He'd climbed well beyond this height before—just not while carrying a backpack, in strong wind and over water.

He gritted his teeth and hauled himself up the rope inch by inch, using his feet as he'd been taught. It wasn't easy in heavy mining boots but soon he was almost at the top.

"How goes it below, 'awkeye?" Scarr's voice came from the Poop deck.

Now what was he to do? He couldn't climb over the railings on the Poop deck with Scarr standing right there! Didn't the man sleep?

Matt's arms ached. Sweat poured down his back and he thought he might fall at any moment. Should he continue and risk being caught, or go back down and try again later? He felt so disheartened. He had no choice but to retreat and hope that he still had the strength to climb the rope later.

It was then that he recalled what Scarr had said about fresh sea air. Was it possible that Scarr's cabin window was still open? Matt lowered himself quietly back onto the jolly boat and leaned over to see. Yes! It looked as though the window in the corner on the starboard side was still ajar.

What if he could hang from the jolly boat on its mooring rope, and get in through the open window? Matt closed his eyes. What was he thinking? It was a crazy idea! He also knew it was his only hope—if he wanted to get out of here any time soon.

Matt reached under the tarp, hauled out the mooring rope and threw it over the edge to make sure that it was long enough. After testing that it was tied securely onto the front of the boat, he took hold and swung his legs over the edge. At that moment he was actually thankful for all of his gym lessons. Mr. Daniels had taught him the proper way to descend without getting rope burns. Now he hoped he had the strength in his arms to lower himself slowly.

But after one minute his arms ached and pain shot through the muscles in his chest. He tightened the grip of his feet on the rope to slow his speed, and used his knees when he had to. He _could_ do this. _Just don't look down at the water_, he told himself.

Matt felt for the window ledge with his right foot. Then, wedging the toe of his boot into the open window he forced it open further, and squeezed himself through the window, landing on a well-worn couch underneath.

Matt exhaled. He'd done it! He looked around Scarr's cabin and groaned, "Can't believe I'm back here."

Just then he heard a loud rumble. The sound was similar to what he'd heard earlier in the day when the anchor was being lowered. The pirates were shouting and Scarr was bellowing commands. It all seemed to point to one thing—the _Dreamseeker_ was setting sail!

Panic gripped him. If Varl and Targon were on the island of Moji, he might never see them again! He had to get out on deck and see what was going on—but dressed like this he'd be spotted instantly. Perhaps he could wear some of the captain's clothes?

Matt looked around the room. Where would Scarr keep clothing? There were no cupboards, pegs or wardrobes that he could see. He walked over to the captain's bunk on the far side of the cabin. At the foot of the bed was an enormous trunk. Matt heaved open the lid and smiled when he saw the container was stuffed full of clothing. But his initial happiness turned to dismay as he sorted through fancy white shirts, knee breeches and dress coats edged with gold braid. Maybe Scarr dressed like this for tourists, but the deck hands certainly didn't! The clothes were useless if he wanted to blend in with the swabbies. He raked the clothes to one side. Surely Scarr had something he could use!

When he found a pair of smelly brown shoes with silver buckles, long brown woolen stockings and some dark green calf-length trousers, he was euphoric. He hurriedly undressed, pulled on the stockings and then the trousers. Zang it! They were too wide around the waist—Scarr was a large man!

He dug deeper in the trunk. All he needed was a belt. He selected a long red sash, and wrapped it tightly around his waist, concealing the top of the trousers and holding them up.

The shoes were uncomfortable, but they would have to do. Now what could he do about a shirt? Matt pulled out one of the fancy white tops and ripped the frills from around the cuffs and the neck. Perfect. A sleeveless red jacket finished the outfit. Finally he looked like one of the swabbies. Matt stuffed his old red garments into his backpack with his computer and closed the lid of the trunk.

He was about to leave the cabin when he caught his reflection in a silver platter on the table. His shiny blond hair was a giveaway! How could he hide it?

Matt opened the trunk one more time and fished around until he found a red and yellow patterned headscarf. But no matter how he positioned it on his head, wisps of blond hair escaped.

He noticed an old quill pen and a bottle of black ink on Scarr's desk. Ink? Not the ideal solution, but it would probably be good enough to hide his sideburns.

Matt gingerly dipped his index finger into the bottle and, using the silver platter as a mirror, did his best to dye his escaping hair. The stain left on his fingertip was a good indication that it would last. He wiped his finger on his pants and picked up his backpack. It didn't go with the rest of his pirate outfit, but for now he dared not part with it. He would just have to do his best to keep it out of sight. He drew in a deep breath and walked to the door. Within minutes he would know if his disguise was good enough.

The cabin door creaked as he opened it. Matt peered through the crack. There was a frenzy of activity on deck. The boatswains were raising the sails, and ropes were being hauled. He could hear the capstan turning and Scarr hollering commands. The *Dreamseeker* would soon be heading out to sea—and there wasn't a thing he could do to stop it.

Chapter 7

"Pueblo Verde," muttered Targon as he followed Gabriela along the well-worn beach path. "What does it mean?"

"Green Village," she said, pointing to the lush vegetation inland. "My village is right on the water's edge. It has a sandy beach and many rocky inlets that are good for fishing, and at the same time the palm trees are tall and provide much-needed shade."

"It sounds like paradise," said Targon. "In Zaul, where I'm from, the trees are in desperate need of water. They cling to the mountainsides, twisted and withered—but they are still beautiful, I think."

The sun was low, glimmering across the rippling sea and painting a magnificent display of pinks and reds across the sky. Targon stopped walking to watch it disappear below the horizon.

"We'll be there in five minutes," said Gabriela.

"Great, because right now I'm so thirsty I could run straight into the water."

Gabriela laughed. "But you wouldn't want to drink it when you got there."

"I've heard that it's salty," said Targon. He could feel his cheeks warm with embarrassment. Why had he just said that? Gabriela must think him stupid.

"Do you live a long way from the sea, then?" she asked with genuine interest.

Targon relaxed when he heard no judgment of him in her voice. "Yes, actually I'd never seen the sea before today," he admitted.

"Then I'll take you down to Devil's Cove tomorrow."

"Devil's Cove? Do I *want* to go there?"

Gabriela laughed. "Don't worry. It's just a nickname my ancestors gave our little beach. But you'll love it. The cove is beautiful and the water is so calm—and you can see the whole of the Bay of Moji from there."

"I can hardly wait," said Targon, trying to hide his nervousness. Would she expect him to be able to swim?

"Well, we'd better get going. It'll get dark very quickly now that the sun has set."

Gabriela set off again, and Targon followed, focusing on the bright yellow flowers printed on her dress, still visible in the near-darkness. His mind returned to Varl. Had he done the right thing by leaving Balamachu? Perhaps he hadn't spent long enough looking for him. What if the old man had crawled into some dark corner that Targon hadn't spotted?

He felt sick to his stomach, torn between his decision to get help and his feelings that he had abandoned his friend. But it was too late now. He'd made the choice and he had to stick with it.

They arrived at a clearing. Gabriela turned away from the sea, and headed toward some lights that flickered in the distance.

"Welcome to Pueblo Verde," she said, taking his hand and leading him through the trees. "It's hard to see the path at night."

Targon's mood brightened as they entered the main street. Under the streetlights he could see the small houses were painted in welcoming colors of pink, yellow and blue, and low white fences separated the gardens. Adults sat on their front porches chatting to neighbors and a few children played on the sidewalks.

He stared at the vehicles parked outside some of the homes. They certainly weren't airbugs like the Govans had used in Level 3 of Matt's game. These vehicles had wheels! He was just wondering how they worked when Gabriela pulled him to one side as one approached. It sped past, its engine noise breaking the tranquility of Pueblo Verde. What loud, dirty things they seemed to be.

"Another hour and everywhere will be quiet," said Gabriela. "The day starts early in Pueblo Verde. The men will be out fishing at dawn."

Targon didn't answer. He was in a trance trying to take in so many new things.

Gabriela stopped outside a large two-story white house with a front porch that wrapped around the sides of the building. It dominated the end of the street. Around the house was a white picket fence, and neatly trimmed shrubs bordered the path up to the front door.

"Welcome to my home," she said, throwing her arms open wide.

"It seems much bigger than everyone else's," Targon remarked.

"It is," she said quietly. "My father, Mowann Kimile, is the Mayor of Moji."

"Really," said Targon.

"He's also the hereditary leader of the Kayapuche tribe and a direct descendent of King Bakana Kimile."

Targon was barely able to control his gasp of surprise. "Is that the same King Bakana Kimile who was married to Queen Elena?"

Gabriela's jaw dropped. "Wow! You know something of my family history. I guess you did some research before you even got to Balamachu." She stared at him with a look of complete astonishment.

Targon shrugged and turned from her scrutiny. "Something like that," he muttered.

"But you don't have to worry," Gabriela added quickly. "My father's just a normal person. I won't let him set the spirits on you, I promise." She laughed gently.

"I assume that's a joke," said Targon, remembering his encounter with the spirit of Queen Elena.

"Of course," said Gabriela. "Now, let's get you a drink of water."

Targon followed her up the steps and through the majestic front door. The enormous marble entrance hall featured a grand staircase with dark wood banisters and a crystal chandelier. He tried not to gape as he walked through the elegant high-ceilinged living room and into a huge kitchen. He thought of his home, where a kitchen this size served everyone who lived in his sector in Zaul. "This whole kitchen is just for your family?" he asked.

She nodded as she handed him a glass of cold water. "Cook will be here bright and early. She'll whip up a breakfast like no other you've ever tasted."

Targon chugged back the water in one go. "Thanks, I needed that. Could I have another, please?"

She had just handed him a refill when a plump black woman with tightly braided hair entered the kitchen.

"*Buenos noches*, Miss Gabriela. *¿Dónde usted ha estado?*—Where *have* you bin?" she said, wagging her finger. "It's dark out and I've bin so worried 'bout you, especially with *su madre* away this week. I feel like I'm responsible for you when your momma's not here."

"I'm sorry to have worried you, Amelia. I only walked over to Balamachu."

"Balamachu! *Dios Mio! En la obscuridad*—in the dark? Thank goodness you're alright!"

Gabriela blushed. "I'm fine, *really*, Amelia. I've brought a friend home with me. Targon, this is Amelia, our wonderful housekeeper."

"Nice to meet you, ma'am."

Amelia smiled at him and then turned her attention back to Gabriela. "*Su padre*—he's mighty angry with you. You missed dinner too. Best you go see your father right now." She wiped her hands on her apron and walked out onto the back porch still muttering, "Balamachu! *Dios Mio!*"

Gabriela called after her, "Thanks, Amelia. I want him

to meet Targon anyway."

"Zang it!" said Targon.

Gabriela smiled. "I've not heard that expression before."

"Your father's not going to be pleased about meeting me if he's already angry with you. Perhaps it would be better if I met him in the morning instead."

She shook her head. "I hope you didn't take me seriously earlier when I was teasing you about spirits. My father's a puppy dog. He wouldn't hurt anyone and he'd do anything for me. There's nothing to worry about—you'll see! He'll be in the study."

Targon followed her back across the entrance hall towards two oak-paneled doors. His stomach churned. No matter what Gabriela had just said, he had a feeling that he wasn't going to enjoy meeting Mowann Kimile.

* * * * *

Matt stood on the Quarterdeck outside of Persivius Scarr's cabin door as the *Dreamseeker* sailed out to sea. He held his scarf on his head in the wind with one hand, and wrapped the other tightly around a rung on the ladder up to the Poop deck. As far as he could tell from the lights on the shore, they were already out of the Bay of Moji and picking up speed.

Billy Rogers was at the helm, using all of his might to turn the wheel. Matt could hear the huge sails billowing in the wind and the bow smacking against the water as she hit the waves full on. His stomach lurched already and they weren't even out to sea. Now was not the time to be seasick. He had to concentrate on something other than the motion of the ship.

Some of the pirates were still up the rigging and just a few were tying off ropes. But as Matt looked down to the Main deck below, something didn't seem to fit with the whole Golden Age pirate picture.

What was that positioned under a black plastic tarp on the Forecastle just above the Main deck? Surely it hadn't been there before or he would have noticed something so large stuck up there. The huge shape on a gigantic metal base could easily be a weapon—like something that might be seen on the top deck of a battleship. In fact, it looked sort of like a . . . what?

"A rocket launcher!" Matt said out loud. What would Scarr need with a rocket launcher? And why had it just appeared on deck?

Matt felt hot as he recalled the captain's words, *"We're pirates, all right—but not as you're thinkin' of pirates. An' let me tell ye, boy, we're still the kind of pirates you wouldn't want to cross."* Whatever Scarr was up to had to tie in with Level 5 of his game. He'd just have to get down to the hold in order to follow up the clues in the first rhyme.

He quickly found the aft steps down to the Gun deck and was about to make his way back across to the tiller room ladder when one of the pirates came up behind him.

"Dinner's up, mate."

"Thanks, mate," Matt mumbled back, his heart racing. He turned to hide his backpack and smiled at the pirate.

"And it's not the usual muck. Cap'n's ordered a feast before tonight's raid."

"Thanks again," Matt mumbled a second time.

"I 'aven't seen ye before. Ye new?"

"Scarr 'ired me yesterday," Matt replied, trying to put on a pirate accent.

"Welcome aboard. Ye came just in time for some excitement."

Matt nodded, but said nothing.

"Anyway, yer'd best get to the kitch'n before it's all gone—and yer'd better get rid of yer pack before Scarr sees yer up 'ere with it."

He watched the pirate disappear up the steps to Main deck and exhaled heavily. What had the man meant by 'tonight's raid'? And why had he told Matt to get rid of his pack? One thing was sure—the backpack was a real problem. But apart from that, his disguise seemed convincing enough. Of course, the real test would come when he had to face someone who already knew him.

Matt arrived in the tiller room and bent his head as he walked under the long pole. There on a stool was a glass of fresh water and a plate piled high with fresh bread, roast beef and salad. Bart the tillerman had obviously been to the kitchen for his dinner. Matt licked his lips. He hadn't realized how hungry he was until that moment. It had been at least twelve hours since he had last eaten.

His stomach growled. He had to eat while he had the opportunity. After all, Bart could get more food easily. Matt wolfed down several pieces of beef and a couple of cherry tomatoes, one after the other, and guzzled half the water.

He was reaching for another piece of beef when the ladder creaked. Bart the tillerman was returning to eat! Matt took the beef and shoved it into his mouth, grabbed several pieces of thick crusty bread and escaped into the surgeon's cockpit, stuffing the bread into the front pocket of his backpack as he ran through the room. But where was the ladder down to the hold? He couldn't face hiding in the cupboard with the rats again—especially not with food!

Matt dashed into the powder room, which was stacked on both sides with barrels. Did Scarr keep them filled with gunpowder? He hoped he wouldn't find out. Against the starboard side was an open trapdoor with steps. That had to be it! He was just heading toward the door when at least fifteen men pushed past him and rushed to the ladder. One by one they descended at speed.

"Out of me way, boy," snapped one. "We're on a tight schedule 'ere."

Matt squeezed himself between two barrels and put his hands on one of them, pretending to check them over.

"Get movin'!" hollered the last man in line. "The anchor's droppin' in seventeen minutes. We've all got to be down there, dressed an' ready to go."

"Loosen up—you're always so uptight!" said the man in front of him.

"Chill, O'Malley!" someone called up from the hold.

Matt frowned. Chill? That word wasn't in any pirate's vocabulary, he was sure. He waited until O'Malley had gone down into the hold and then knelt on the floor, trying to get a glimpse through the hatch. But he couldn't see anything below.

"Boy!"

Matt wheeled around in panic.

Bart the tillerman was standing over him. "Take this to Conan O'Malley. Tell him Scarr says there's a definite target onboard—'e's in stateroom 1004." He handed him a small thin cylinder, the size of a pen, with a flashing red light embedded in one end.

Matt nodded, a lump rising in his throat as he saw Bart staring at him. If anyone would recognize him it would be the tillerman. He took the gadget from Bart's hands, trying not to shake. Bart suddenly frowned and said, "Best get back to me dinner—what's left of it. Those idiots think they can pinch me food—second time this week." He walked away muttering.

Matt realized his back was wet with perspiration. He closed his eyes and breathed deeply. That had been too close! But now he had the excuse he needed to enter the hold.

Chapter 8

Targon swallowed hard as Gabriela opened the enormous study doors. She caught hold of his sleeve and pulled him into the room. Targon was staggered by the number of books that filled the shelves from floor to ceiling on two walls—it was a small library! At the ends of some of the shelves were elegant bronze statues that served as bookends. The room smelled of education and wealth.

Mowann Kimile, a big, dark-haired and powerful-looking man, was sat behind a large wooden desk with his back to the windows. He was talking on a small wireless phone, leafing through a pile of official-looking documents and occasionally glancing at two computer screens in front of him. He looked up over the top of his gold-rimmed glasses and smiled broadly when he realized it was his daughter. He immediately finished his call and put the paperwork down, beaming with pride as Gabriela approached. Targon instantly liked him.

"Gabriela, my dear," he said, pushing back his chair and rising. "I was getting concerned for your well-being. It's not like you to miss dinner."

Gabriela walked round his desk and kissed him on the cheek. "Father, you needn't have worried—you know I can look after myself."

Mowann Kimile turned off one of his computer screens and put his glasses down on the desk. He took her by the shoulders and looked her squarely in the eyes. His expression lost its warmth and became serious. "That may be the case, but I've decided I don't want you wandering around Moji on your own, particularly while it's summer and with so many tourists on the island. I shall start interviewing for bodyguards tomorrow and you'll have one by the end of the week."

Gabriela groaned. "Please, Father, there's no need for that. I promise I'll be back before dusk every night."

"I'm sorry, Mr. Kimile," Targon interrupted. "It's really my fault that Gabriela is late. You see, I got separated from my friends at Balamachu and Gabriela offered to help me find them."

Mowann Kimile came around his desk and stood in front of Targon, towering over him. A cold expression settled on his face. "And who might you be?"

"Targon." He managed a tremulous smile and added, "sir."

"Targon. *Just* Targon?"

Targon shifted uneasily. Perhaps he didn't like this man after all. "Targon Hammond," he said quickly, using Matt's last name since he didn't have one of his own.

"Targon Hammond," he repeated in a deep, stern voice. "And where are you from, Targon Hammond?"

"Er, Z . . . Z . . . Zaul, sir," he stammered, realizing that he couldn't change the story he gave Gabriela.

"And where exactly is Zaul?" Mowann Kimile

continued to interrogate.

"It's a small kingdom bordering the Empire of Gova and the Colony of Javeer," replied Targon, not knowing what else to say. Truthfully, he had no idea where Zaul was—or anywhere else he had traveled with Matt. Mowann Kimile's eyebrows shot up as if he were totally dumbfounded. "Oh, really."

There was an awkward silence. Targon smiled to himself. It was obvious that Mowann Kimile did not want to look stupid and admit that he had no idea where these places were. And for the first time Targon wondered if he was still in his own time period, 2540 AD. Every level of Matt's computer game was supposed to take place on Earth in 2540 AD—even though Matt was actually from 2010. But he'd seen pirates dressed in clothing from centuries past and Gabriela's house wasn't exactly full of sophisticated technology. So perhaps this wasn't 2540 after all.

"And what are you doing on Moji?" Mowann Kimile finally continued.

"I came with my two friends for a vacation and to study your pyramids," said Targon, suddenly proud of his ability to fabricate a story. "Matt is a boy my age and Varl is a great scientist and historian. He told me a lot about the ancient burial tombs and stucco friezes here on Moji."

"I see," said Mowann Kimile. He folded his arms and cleared his throat. "You seem young to be interested in such things. How old are you, Targon?"

"Thirteen, I think."

"You *think*?" he countered.

Targon broke out in a cold sweat. How could he have been so stupid to slip up like that? "No, I mean, thirteen, sir. I *am* thirteen." He wondered if he had succeeded in convincing the man and decided to add, "It's just that my birthday is soon and I've lost track of today's date with being on vacation. So I could be fourteen by now."

Targon thought he could see a glint of amusement in Mowann Kimile's eyes.

"It's September 30th," said Gabriela quickly, as if she were trying to rescue him from his embarrassment.

"September 30th of what year?" asked Targon.

"2540, of course," said Gabriela, laughing. "How long do you think you've been on vacation?"

"Just teasing you," said Targon quickly.

Much to Targon's surprise Mowann Kimile laughed too. "Okay, enough with the questions," he said, softening. "I just like to know about my daughter's friends. I'm sure you understand."

Targon nodded. "Of course, sir."

"Right, well, let's get down to business. Pull up a chair, both of you."

"Business?" asked Targon.

"Your lost friends. If Gabriela thinks you are worth helping, then I'd like to be of help too. And since Cook has already gone for the night, I'll get Amelia to make us some sandwiches."

"Thank you," said Targon.

"If anyone can find your friends, I can."

Targon smiled at him, but his stomach was in knots. At least he knew that it was still 2540. But could he tell Mowann Kimile about what had happened to Varl at Balamachu? Would the man believe him? And as for Matt—what story could he possibly spin there? After all, he was only guessing that Matt was on a pirate ship—he didn't actually know that for sure.

* * * * *

Matt recited the rhyme in his head as he climbed down the ladder into the hold. *Below Orlop deck you will find this pirate ship's not of its kind.* And what was that line about finding the mutineers? It seemed as though everyone onboard was happy—everyone except O'Malley. He'd have to watch and listen more closely from now on.

Matt reached the bottom of the ladder and turned around. His eyes widened and he had to stop himself from shouting with the shock of what he saw. It was as if he had entered another world. Suddenly the dark dingy surroundings of a 17th century ship had disappeared, replaced by a gleaming futuristic-looking underwater laboratory.

"2540 AD," Matt muttered. "Why didn't I think about that before?" Every level in his *Keeper of the Kingdom* game was supposed to take place in 2540 AD. He had really lost sight of that fact by being onboard a 17th century sailing ship. And even when he had seen a motorboat, cruise ship and tourists it seemed as though he were still in his own time. Finally he knew he was in the right place, playing his game.

Matt looked around in awe. The hull of the pirate ship had been completely transformed to accommodate a large rectangular airlock that filled the center of the vessel. It was plainly in view through some kind of thick transparent material that formed the walls. The top of the airlock was level with a built-up platform at least four feet high. Matt could see the edges of the airlock doors protruding from each side of the platform. There was little room to walk around the edge.

Floating in the airlock were two sleek, white mini-subs, each with thin wings and a turret that protruded several feet above the main body in the middle of the craft. On each side of the turret was one large round porthole, and several smaller ones were down the sides of the main body. Mounted on the top of the turret was a smaller version of the rocket launcher that Matt had seen earlier on the Forecastle.

The complete bow of the hold was raised another foot above the level of the platform. In the bow three men sat at control panels watching radar and several gigantic computer screens.

Matt noticed that none of the men walking around the hold was dressed in pirate costumes. Instead the crew were wearing black jumpsuits, knee-high black boots, and elbow-length leather gloves with silver studs. These men looked to him like high-tech bikers. Each carried a black helmet with a dark acrylic visor, making them look even more like bikers. It seemed strange that so many men were all dressed *exactly* alike.

And as Matt studied their accessories he suddenly realized that each carried a backpack very similar to his own! Now he understood why the pirate on the Gun deck had told him to get rid of the backpack before Scarr saw him. What were these men about to do?

"You supposed to be down here, boy?" asked one of the men. His demeanor was threatening.

"Er, yes," said Matt, who had been so preoccupied with his new surroundings that he hadn't noticed him approach. "I 'ave a message for Conan O'Malley from Cap'n Scarr." At least he had a genuine reason for being there.

"Okay. I'll get him." The man backed away and shouted, "Hey! O'Malley! You're wanted."

Conan O'Malley smoothed back his thick black hair as he approached. Even though the pirates around him were also clad in black, O'Malley's tall, well-groomed appearance seemed out of place. He visibly stiffened. "This had better be good," he snarled in a deep voice.

Matt handed him the pen-like device. Now what was it he was supposed to say? "Message from Cap'n Scarr. 'e says there's a definite target onboard—'e's in stateroom 1004."

"You've done your job," said O'Malley, his mouth twisting into a sneer. "Now get out of here!"

O'Malley's appearance may be of place, but his

attitude sure isn't, thought Matt. He reluctantly put one foot on the bottom rung of the ladder, realizing that there was no way he could stay down there unnoticed. Suddenly O'Malley grabbed him by the shoulder.

"Change of plan," he said. "You've just been recruited!"

"'ow do you mean?" said Matt, totally bewildered by this sudden reversal of position.

"And you can start by losing the phony pirate accent when you're down here in the hold."

"I can?" said Matt, unsure what that meant.

"Scarr won't miss a cabin boy for a few hours."

"Probably not," he said.

"Good. We're a man short. P. J.'s just got sick—some virus or other. You're taking his place tonight—we don't have time to get anyone else."

"*I'm* taking his place?" said Matt. "Doing what?"

O'Malley shot him a dirty look. "As if you didn't know."

"I do know. I just mean *what* will I be doing, *exactly*?"

"You can climb a rope ladder, right?"

"Sure," said Matt. Climbing a rope ladder sounded easy after what he'd just gone through climbing a rope to get into Scarr's cabin from the jolly boat.

"Good. That's settled, then. That's all you need to know for now. We'd better get you kitted up. Go to the clothing storeroom." He pointed to a door in the stern. "You'll need a jumpsuit, gloves and boots. You'll need a helmet too. Find P.J.'s locker. We don't have any spare helmets, so we'll just have to hope your head is the same size as his."

"Okay," said Matt.

"Oh, and I can see you have a backpack already."

"Scarr gave me one for an errand I had to run," lied Matt.

"Fine. You've only got eleven minutes until launch so you'd better make it snappy."

Matt hurried from the ladder into the stern. He wasn't sure quite what he was getting himself into, but wasn't this the best way to find out what Scarr was up to?

Matt passed the lockers and entered the clothing store that O'Malley had pointed to. Cubbyholes along the sides of the ship were filled with jumpsuits, gloves and other items. A short bench was bolted to the floor in the middle.

Matt sorted through the collection of jumpsuits until he found one his size. When he was completely dressed he found P.J.'s locker, and pulled out the helmet. It wasn't a snug fit, but at least it would hide his blond hair.

Now what should he do about his computer? Matt debated leaving it in P.J.'s locker, but thought better of it. He couldn't risk it being found. It would have to stay in his backpack. However, he removed his old red clothing and shoved it in the locker along with his pirate clothes, in case he needed more room in the backpack.

As he walked over to where O'Malley stood by the first mini-sub, his heart raced. He remembered how claustrophobic he had felt on his last submarine adventure. But it was too late to turn back.

Chapter 9

Varl groaned. His head throbbed so hard he thought his brain might explode. He could see fuzzy shapes as they faded in and out of his vision. He could hear people's voices, but he couldn't make out how many people were in the room or what they were saying. Where was he?

He tried to sit up, but his hands seemed to be tied to the bed. Panic-struck, he snatched his arms back and forth against the ropes in an effort to free himself.

Someone bent over him. "Be still," the voice whispered in his ear.

Then he felt a jab in his arm.

* * * * *

"Pirates!" said Targon, deciding the truth was his best bet where Mowann Kimile was concerned. "You have to believe me, they were pirates. I even heard their names—Skimmy McFinn and Billy Rogers. I watched them push my friend, Varl, down the steps of Balamachu!"

"Oh, how awful!" said Gabriela, her mouth agape.

"It was horrible," continued Targon. "I was sick to my

stomach. Varl was unconscious at the bottom of the steps and he was bleeding badly from his head. But then, only a few minutes later, he was gone! It was as if he'd just vanished into thin air."

"Hmm," grunted Mowann Kimile. "And when did this all supposedly happen?"

Targon sighed. "*Supposedly?* I knew you wouldn't believe me."

Mowann Kimile shifted uncomfortably in his chair. "I said *supposedly* because I'm just trying to put together a timeline for all of these events."

"It happened earlier today—this afternoon . . . mid-afternoon," said Targon.

"Okay. I'll see what I can find out. Actually, I've heard of McFinn and Rogers."

"You have?" said Targon. "So you've dealt with pirates before?"

"The island of Moji and many other islands in this area have been home to pirates for centuries. There is, unfortunately, a very strong pirate element on Moji at the moment."

Mowann Kimile glanced at his daughter. Targon got the distinct feeling that he was choosing his words carefully for her benefit. Perhaps he didn't want to scare her, or perhaps there were things about the pirates that he didn't want her to know. After seeing the treasure stashed in Mowann Kimile's family tomb, Targon couldn't help but wonder if Gabriela's father knew the pirates were using the tomb to stash their booty. But for the moment he'd keep that fact to himself.

"I and other lawmakers have been trying to eradicate this latest band who have chosen our shores. But as you can see, Targon, they are evil men with weapons at their disposal, and we have had to be careful how we act so as not to endanger our citizens."

"So have you met these pirates, Father?" asked Gabriela.

"No, I'm happy to say, I have not. However, I know of their raids and I know that they use our island to stash their booty."

"And I'll bet I know where," said Targon. "Balamachu. It's the perfect place."

"Balamachu?" Mowann Kimile's expression changed and he seemed alarmed by Targon's response. "What exactly *did* you see down there?" he asked slowly.

Targon gulped. Why had he been so careless as to blurt that out? But it was too late to retract what he had said. So carefully he explained about how he had talked to the spirit of Queen Elena.

Mowann Kimile began to sweat profusely. He patted his brow with his handkerchief. "Spirits? That's just an old folk tale. The locals spread the stories of spirits because it helps to preserve the private tombs by keeping the tourists away from them. I've been inside Balamachu hundreds of times and never once seen any spirits."

"I wasn't hallucinating," said Targon indignantly.

"Okay, let's suppose you weren't hallucinating," Kimile snapped. "Did this spirit allow you to enter the tomb? Did you see anything more?"

Targon felt suddenly scared by the tone of Kimile's response and decided to go no further, convinced that Gabriela's father knew about the pirate booty. For now he wouldn't tell them he'd seen what was in the tomb.

"I didn't know the password," he replied. "The spirit of Queen Elena wouldn't let me enter."

"Password? What absolute gobbledygook!" Mowann Kimile yelled. "So you are just *hypothesizing* that the pirates could stash their booty in my family tomb."

"Well, the pirates were at Balamachu, weren't they?" said Targon, to cover his tracks.

Mowann Kimile adjusted his glasses, and let out a deep sigh as if he were trying to calm himself. In a more subdued tone he asked, "What did the two pirates do after they pushed your friend, Varl, down the stairs?"

"They kicked him and left him there to bleed to death."

Gabriela gasped. "That's disgusting!"

"Indeed. It's criminal," said Mowann Kimile. He paused and asked, "What did you do after the pirates left and during the time that Varl disappeared?"

Targon could feel his heart racing. This was a difficult question to answer without revealing the truth. "I was trying to find a light so that I could help Varl. It was so dark down there—I was hoping that I might find a lamp on one of the walls. So I felt my way around the area at the base of the steps. I only had my back turned for five minutes."

"Did you hear anything or anyone?"

"No. Not a thing."

"And what of your other friend, the boy your age?" asked Kimile.

Targon decided he could be truthful here. "The pirates were talking about a blond boy onboard their ship. So I'm guessing they caught him and took him prisoner."

"Really?" said Kimile, raising his voice again. "And why would they do that?"

What did Mowann Kimile know that he wasn't saying? "I thought pirates often took captives," Targon countered.

Kimile said nothing.

"You *will* help Targon, won't you, Father?" pleaded Gabriela.

"We'll send out a search party first thing in the morning, I promise," Mowann Kimile replied, his sympathetic tone sounding put-on.

"And you'll start at Balamachu, right?" said Gabriela.

Mowann Kimile ignored his daughter's question. "I think you should both get a good night's sleep."

Targon decided that he should play along with Kimile's act so he got up and shook his hand firmly. "Thank you, sir. Thank you for agreeing to help."

Gabriela kissed her father on the cheek. "Thanks, Father."

"Not a problem," he said, motioning them to leave. "Now if you'll excuse me, I must make a few calls."

Targon watched Mowann Kimile open his drawer and

take out a small device that looked like a cell phone—but it wasn't the cell phone that he had seen him using earlier.

"What time is it?" Targon asked Gabriela as she closed the study doors.

She looked at her watch. "Nearly midnight."

"It's a bit late for your father to be making calls, isn't it?"

"My father wastes no time. He's probably already making inquiries about your friends."

"That would be really great," said Targon, although he suspected that her father was doing nothing of the kind. Targon was not good at reading books but he could read people, and as far as he was concerned, Mowann Kimile knew much more about the pirates than he had told them.

* * * * *

"Here," said O'Malley. He handed Matt a small black gun. "You might need it."

A gun? What do I know about guns? Matt's hands shook as he examined the weapon. Suddenly he felt very stupid to have put himself in this position. He prayed that nobody was going to get hurt, but that's not what pirates were about, was it? What had he been thinking? This was not going to be some vacation scuba adventure. He'd heard several pirates talking about going on a raid. What had he thought that meant? And now he was going on the raid too. He was glad that the helmet hid his fear.

"Does it have b . . . bu . . . bullets?" Matt asked.

O'Malley laughed. "They went out with the square-rigger! Where have you been for the last hundred years? You're holding an EPE."

"Oh, yes, I've heard of those," bluffed Matt. "How do they work, again?"

O'Malley sighed and grabbed the EPE from him. "It's an Electrical Pulse Emitter. It's just an updated version of electrical weapons that have been around for years. The power supply is here—just press this to send a pulse—and it has an insulated grip to protect you when you're using it."

"What's that button?" asked Matt.

"It's called a dead-man switch. It'll shut off the current. This slider here will change the power level."

Matt gulped. "How powerful is it?"

"It delivers a neuro-current which disrupts nerve impulses. It won't kill—just cause severe pain and temporary paralysis. The effects wear off quickly but the EPE will give you enough time to restrain the victim."

"So it won't kill anyone," repeated Matt, relieved.

"Don't worry, there are torpedo and rocket launchers in the mini-subs and onboard the *Dreamseeker*. That will be enough incentive for our target to cooperate. You won't *need* to kill anyone."

Matt swallowed hard. Even if the weapon couldn't kill, he really did not want any part of this raid. What if something went wrong? Would they blow up the target?

A siren blasted a long screeching tone followed by a softer shorter one. It was so loud that Matt was glad he was wearing a helmet, but it still sent chills up his spine. He always associated sirens with something perilous, and he wondered if today was any different.

"Two-minute warning," mouthed O'Malley.

Matt nodded. He lined up with the other men on the port side of each airlock. Ten men stood in front of each submarine.

"I'll make sure you're okay," said O'Malley, his tone softening a little. It was as if he could sense Matt's apprehension.

"Your first raid?" asked the man in front.

"He's just filling in for P.J.," O'Malley answered.

The seconds ticked by. Matt's heart thudded. He watched O'Malley hold up ten fingers, then nine, eight . . . counting down to what?

"Go!" shouted O'Malley.

Matt found himself swept along with the other nine men. They charged for the mini-sub and dived through the hatch. *This is going to be bad*, thought Matt. Ten of us crammed into each of these tiny subs?

But inside there was more room than he had anticipated. Four men sat on each of two benches, while O'Malley and another man took seats in the turret at the controls. They each wore headsets and seemed absorbed by what was being said to them.

"Everyone in?" asked O'Malley. "We're a go. Strap up."

Matt found his belt and strapped himself in. The siren blasted three long tones.

"Closing inner airlock doors," said O'Malley.

Matt looked up through the window behind his seat. He could just see two huge metal doors moving into position to close off the airlock. There was a loud clunk.

"Opening outer airlock doors," said O'Malley.

Matt could hear grating metal and the mini-sub seemed to bounce in the water momentarily.

"We've been cleared to go," shouted O'Malley.

There was a loud *whoosh!* Matt grabbed onto his seat. It was as if he'd been propelled into space with mind-boggling velocity. His teeth chattered and the flesh on his cheeks flapped. The mini-sub was zooming through the water at an unbelievable speed.

"Twenty miles to target," said O'Malley. "Everyone okay back there?"

The men nodded and grunted in response, but seemed very calm. Matt wanted to ask where they were going, but couldn't. He knew he'd soon find out anyway.

"Ten miles and closing," said O'Malley. "Team leader in sub 1 is contacting target now."

The men beside Matt suddenly sprang to life and the calmness onboard seemed to evaporate. They squirmed in their seats, adjusted their helmets, checked their guns and tugged at their long gloves. Some even did stretching exercises. He wondered if he should be doing the same.

"Approaching target. Floodlights on. Team leader reports captain of target ready to accept terms. Surfacing now."

Matt understood O'Malley's last comment. This was no underwater mission after all. The sub broke the surface and he gasped as he looked through the window and saw that they were pulling up alongside an enormous cruise ship.

Suddenly the mini-sub cut its engines and the hatch flew open.

"Everyone out!" bellowed O'Malley.

The men got to their feet, pushing Matt into the line for the hatch. He poked his head through the hole to find a rope ladder dangling in front of him.

"Grab hold of one of the lower rungs and climb," shouted O'Malley, who was right on his heels.

It was only as the ladder started to sway back and forth, several feet at a time, that Matt realized he was climbing up the side of the cruise ship!

He paused and looked down. One of the pirates held the rocket launcher, which was aimed at the bridge of the cruise ship. Another pirate in the turret was also staying behind, presumably to control the mini-sub. Now Matt understood. Scarr and his crew were tour guides by day and pirates by night, raiding not 17th century galleons but cruise ships of their own time period. And who would have guessed that a vessel such as the *Dreamseeker* could conceal the base for such raids?

"Hey, get a move on!" bellowed O'Malley. "We haven't got all night, you know!"

Matt climbed as fast as he could, battling the stiff sea

breeze and the movement of the ocean. When he landed on deck he copied the man in front and drew his gun. What was he doing? He wasn't about to use it!

"This way." O'Malley climbed over the side and led him along the deck towards the stern.

Matt turned to look at what the other six pirates were doing.

"Forget them," said O'Malley, tugging at his sleeve. "They'll look after the captain and the crew, and they've other things to do onboard. We've got a set target and we've no time for you to be dragging your feet."

The set target's in stateroom 1004, thought Matt, and his stomach churned. Who was the target and were they going to hurt this person? He wished he could turn and run. But run where? The pirates would kill him before he could tell anyone anything. Besides, he had to finish this level of his game if he ever wanted to get home.

"We'll take the elevator down two decks," said O'Malley.

Matt stood in silence in the elevator, still thankful he was able to hide behind the helmet.

As the doors opened O'Malley pulled out his EPE and ran down the corridor. Matt followed, pretending to be a willing participant.

Once they were standing outside suite 1004, O'Malley pulled out the small pen-like object that Matt had given him and held it up high. The little red light flashed on the top. "Good, our target is in his room. That makes things easy. You ready?"

Matt nodded, although he didn't think he'd ever be ready for something like this.

O'Malley motioned to Matt to stand to one side of the door. Then he knocked gently and said, "Room service."

A man with a deep voice shouted back. "There must be some mistake. We're dining with the captain tonight."

"This was ordered by your wife, sir," pressed O'Malley.

Matt heard the lock click. O'Malley stood hard against the wall. The door opened slowly.

A balding man in a dark dinner jacket peered round the door saying, "But my wife and children have already gone down to the restaurant—"

He had hardly finished his sentence when O'Malley rushed through the door, pushing him backwards and pinning him against the cabin wall. "Senator," he said in a cool, commanding voice. "If you know what's good for you and your family you will cooperate with my demands and you won't do anything foolish."

"W . . . w . . . what is it you . . . you want?" stammered the senator.

O'Malley beckoned to Matt. "Come here and watch him."

Matt felt sick. *Please do as he says, Senator,* he thought as he pointed the EPE at him. This was a nightmare.

O'Malley walked over to the closet and opened the door. "Give me the combination to the cabin safe."

"5692," mumbled the senator.

"Louder!" snapped O'Malley.

"5692," repeated the senator more forcefully.

O'Malley pulled out a huge wad of crisp bills and several large velvet boxes. He flicked through the bills. "Nice of you to carry so much cash with you," he said sarcastically. He opened one of the velvet boxes and laughed.

"Please, not my wife's diamonds," the senator begged. "They're worth millions."

"Then it's a pity she didn't put them on tonight," said O'Malley. "But I guess she's wearing something just as valuable." He filled a clear plastic bag from his backpack with everything in the safe, tied it securely and slammed the closet door closed. "Face down on the floor and hands behind your back!" he ordered, moving Matt to one side.

The senator struggled onto his knees and then fell flat on the carpet. "Please . . ." he begged.

"Just shut up and you won't be hurt," said O'Malley. He took a beeping metal device out of his backpack and clamped it around the senator's hands. "In thirty minutes the beeping will stop. If you attempt to remove the clamp before the beeping stops, it will explode. Do you understand, Senator?"

The senator mumbled, "Yes."

O'Malley forced the plastic bag into his backpack and turned to Matt. "Right, let's get out of here."

Matt had never exited a room so fast in his life. He just wanted this to be over. O'Malley charged up two flights of stairs, turning occasionally to check that Matt was still behind him. Finally they reached the others who had congregated back on deck. Their backpacks were bulging and large plastic bags filled with cash were thrown over their shoulders.

"Okay, the captain knows that if he contacts the authorities in the next thirty minutes his ship will be blown out of the water," said O'Malley. "So let's not waste any time getting off this baby and back to the *Dreamseeker*."

Matt's head was spinning as he climbed over the side and onto the ladder. Going down was just as difficult as going up had been. The ladder seemed to have a mind of its own, twisting against his body movements, and the windy conditions weren't helping.

When Matt finally sat down in the mini-sub he had never felt such relief, even if it meant he was going back to the *Dreamseeker*. He just couldn't forget the senator's frightened expression as he'd waved the EPE in his face. He never wanted to threaten anyone ever again. Thank goodness nobody had been hurt.

As the mini-sub raced back to the square-rigger, Matt was going over the rhyme in his mind and making plans. He knew that he had to deactivate the Keeper—or did the rhyme say Keepers? Was there more than one Keeper to destroy, as there had been in Level 4 of his game? But the first step was to find out who onboard might turn against Captain Persivius Scarr and help him.

Chapter 10

Yarl opened his eyes. Once again his vision was foggy, but this time after a few minutes he was able to focus. A sharp pain shot from his forehead to his ears. He wanted to grab his head, but as he tried to move his hands and then his legs he realized that they were tied to the bed. Hadn't he attempted to get off the bed once before? But now he didn't feel panicked by his restraint—in fact, he felt remarkably calm. Perhaps he had been drugged and the effects hadn't completely worn off.

He turned his head slowly toward the source of the light. It was a small open window with bright green curtains that were fluttering in the balmy breeze. He breathed in deeply. Sea air. He obviously wasn't in Zaul. But where was he?

"Help!" he yelled. "Someone help me! Is anyone there?"

But all he heard was the wind in the trees.

* * * * *

It was barely dawn when Targon dressed and made his way down to the kitchen. His stomach rumbled.

Whatever was cooking smelled divine. Cook was obviously already hard at work preparing breakfast. He sidled up to the stove and tried to see what was sizzling in the skillet, but she ordered him into the dining room. He sat down at the long formal table, which was covered with a white lace tablecloth and elegantly set with silver cutlery. He unfolded his napkin and spread it across his lap. He felt as though he should sit upright at such a table. But after a few minutes his eyelids drooped and he slumped in the chair. He hadn't slept well. How could he? Varl was missing and he had no idea where Matt was.

"You're up early," said Gabriela as she walked into the dining room and sat down opposite him.

Targon yawned. "I couldn't sleep."

"Neither could I—too much excitement yesterday."

Targon looked up. How could she be so bright and awake? She looked so pretty dressed in pink shorts, with a pink flower elegantly placed in the knot of thick hair on top of her head.

Cook waltzed in with two perfectly cooked fluffy omelets and placed one in front of him. The fabulous smell had been killing him and he couldn't wait any longer. He picked up his fork and dug in ravenously before Gabriela had hers.

"So where shall we start looking?" Gabriela asked when Cook was out of sight.

"I'm glad to hear you say that," said Targon. "I thought that you might want to leave it to your father."

She shook her head. "Father's very busy. I'm sure he'll do his best to find your friends, but why waste time? I've nothing to do today, anyway."

"Thanks, Gabriela. I was planning on going back to Balamachu."

"It's as good a place as any to start looking. Perhaps you can conjure up the spirit again," she laughed and then stopped abruptly—presumably because Targon wasn't laughing.

He said nothing. Until she saw the spirit of Queen Elena, she'd never believe him.

Mowann Kimile appeared at the dining room door, a cell phone in one hand and a briefcase in the other.

"Morning, Father," said Gabriela. She blew him a kiss.

"Morning, you two. I just wanted to let you know, Targon, that I've got people out looking for your friends."

"Thank you, sir," said Targon.

Mowann Kimile's cell phone rang. "Sorry, I'll have to take this. I'll see you both at dinner tonight."

After the front door closed Targon said, "So, are we still going to Balamachu?"

"Of course," said Gabriela. "And then perhaps I can take you down to Devil's Cove this afternoon."

"I'd like that."

"I'll get us a few supplies and see you outside in a minute."

Targon wolfed down his omelet, took their plates into the kitchen and thanked Cook. He walked out of the kitchen door and into the early morning sunshine. For the first time in hours he felt optimistic.

Gabriela greeted him with a smile. She had a brightly patterned canvas bag on a long strap slung over her right shoulder. "Okay, we're all set. I've plenty of water for you!"

"Thanks," said Targon. "I'm not used to this heat."

They strolled along the coastal path. It was a refreshing walk. The sky was clear blue with a few wispy clouds and there was a gentle tropical breeze. He tried to enjoy the scenery, but he kept thinking of Varl.

They approached Balamachu from a different direction, scrambling up a grassy bank to get to the base of the pyramid.

"Are there any other pyramids around here that Varl might have gone to?" asked Targon.

"There are four smaller ones nearby—all part of the old city of Balamachu and all on my father's land. Three of them are no more than a pile of stones covered in moss. My father closed the fourth one off last year because the steps were crumbling so badly. Look, you can see it." She pointed to the north.

"Oh, yes," said Targon. "Well, I guess we'll have to think again if we don't find anything here."

Gabriela made climbing to the top of Balamachu look easy. Targon marveled at how nimble and athletic she was, and he followed her up without thinking about the crumbling steps.

As they started down into the tomb, Gabriela

produced a flashlight from her bag. Targon's heart raced. What if they found Varl dead at the bottom of the steps? What if he'd been there all along, lying alone in the darkness?

Gabriela reached the bottom of the steps first and walked around, shining the flashlight into every corner of the tomb.

"I don't see him," she said. "Where exactly did you say he was?"

"Right here," said Targon, kneeling on the floor. He touched the ground with the palm of his hand. "Shine the flashlight, will you?"

Gabriela knelt beside him and focused the beam on the ground. "What are you looking for?" she asked.

"Anything. Anything at all. Just a sign that Varl was here."

"Like this?" she said, pointing to a dark patch on the stones.

"Do you think it's Varl's blood?"

"Hard to tell in this light, but I think it could be."

"Well, at least that shows I wasn't going mad."

"I do believe you," she said. "But the spirit of Queen Elena hasn't appeared, and that's a pity."

Targon was disappointed too. He'd hoped to prove to Gabriela that he hadn't been seeing things. Wait a minute! He could show her the booty! "Shine the light into the tomb," he said excitedly.

Gabriela shone the flashlight through the gate. Targon pressed his face up against the bars and strained to see into the dark cavern beyond. He gasped. There was nothing there! Where was the gold, the money and the jewelry? And where were the crates? What had happened to everything? He banged his head against the bars in frustration.

"What's the matter?" asked Gabriela.

"Nothing," he said. What was the point of telling her? At least she believed what he had said about Varl.

* * * * *

Matt waited for the mini-sub to dock and the inner airlock doors to open, his apprehension increasing. He would have to change back into his pirate clothes without anyone recognizing him. As long as he didn't run into Skimmy McFinn, Billy Rogers, Bart the tillerman, Hawkeye or Scarr, he stood a chance of getting away with it.

He pushed his way in front of the others so that he was first out of the mini-sub, and raced round to the lockers, hoping to change clothing before the other pirates arrived. He was already out of the black jumpsuit and was pulling on Scarr's torn white shirt when O'Malley opened the locker next to him.

"We're done for the night," said O'Malley. "Or should I say morning. Breakfast will be ready for us."

"Great," said Matt, happy that he'd have more to eat than the pieces of bread in his backpack.

"You *can* take your helmet off now," said O'Malley.

"Yes, sure," said Matt, quickly reaching into P.J.'s locker for his headscarf.

When O'Malley bent down to remove his boots, Matt ducked behind the locker door, switched the helmet for the scarf and picked up his backpack. *Whew! That was close!*

O'Malley stood up and stared at him. Matt knew instantly that he was in trouble. *Zang it!* he thought, fumbling to conceal the strands of blond hair that he could feel escaping from under the scarf.

O'Malley grabbed him by the arm and pulled him into the storeroom. He closed the door and let go of Matt's arm. "You're the boy that was in the jolly boat this morning, aren't you?" he whispered.

Matt's nerves tensed immediately. He nodded slowly.

"You've got some explaining to do—and I don't want any lies. What's with the disguise and the blackened sideburns? I want the truth and nothing but the truth—got it?"

Matt blinked, baffled. Why hadn't O'Malley sounded the alarm instantly—and why was he whispering? Could O'Malley be one of the mutineers that his rhyme had talked of? What should he tell this man? The truth about his computer game would seem like a fabrication, but he had to find the mutineers. "I'm on a mission," he finally admitted in a low voice.

"A mission? Is this some kind of kid's game to see how long you can stay onboard without getting caught?"

Matt shook his head. O'Malley had touched on the

truth, but it was time to take a calculated risk. "No, this is for real. I'm here to infiltrate Scarr's organization."

O'Malley looked stunned, and Matt knew it was one truth he had not been expecting.

"But you're just a teenager!" O'Malley said in a forced whisper. Something in his pocket beeped. He reached his hand inside and said, "I'll be back in ten minutes. Don't go anywhere or I'll turn you over to Scarr! You'll be safe here. Do you understand?"

Matt nodded. As the door closed he let out a long sigh. He sat down on an old bench, quickly opened his backpack and took out his laptop. He had to find out as much as he could about Conan O'Malley before the man returned.

The menu quickly appeared and Matt scrolled through his choices. He clicked on Number 3, *Mutineers.*

A scene appeared with pirates wielding cutlasses in time to swashbuckling music. And then the husky pirate voice returned to read the second rhyme.

This time help comes from two sides
Because you're playing Level 5
Among Scarr's hand-picked motley crew
Are infiltrators just like you
Scarr's raids are not for wealth or fame
His booty's for a dangerous game
But many governments are aware
Against attack they must prepare
So once onboard ask for a shield

To find best agents in their field
On Moji locate and persuade
The islanders that you must save
To work with you against the state
To wipe out pirates—it's not too late.

Matt was overjoyed. The rhyme was much longer than usual, contained a lot of information and seemed to confirm what he already suspected. The words *infiltrators* and *agents* convinced him that he had to trust Conan O'Malley. After all, the man *had* seemed different from the other pirates. He read the rhyme again.

He'd assumed that Scarr was raiding cruise ships for the money and the notoriety of being a pirate, but the rhyme told him otherwise. So what exactly should he tell O'Malley about his mission? He needed to know more about the two Keepers of the Island in order to convince O'Malley to work with him. But it was too late. The door was opening. Matt closed the lid of his laptop.

O'Malley looked over his shoulder as he entered the room—another good sign that this man could be trusted, Matt thought.

"Okay, where were we?" O'Malley said, his eyes focusing on the computer. "And what's that on your lap?"

"First, agent Conan O'Malley, I'd like to see your shield."

O'Malley's jaw dropped. Then his eyes narrowed. "Where did you get that information?"

"I told you I'm on a mission. I have my sources just

like you do."

O'Malley froze. He seemed unsure as to his next move, but then he slowly reached into the top pocket of his jumpsuit and produced a leather wallet. He opened it to reveal a small golden star. "There. Satisfied? I don't know who you are, or who you represent, but you aren't leaving this room until I find out!"

"I understand that you're confused and concerned," Matt replied, trying to sound like an adult. "But I think that we're both after the same thing—the downfall of Persivius Scarr. It would be beneficial for us to work together."

O'Malley glowered at him. "Just drop the act, kid! One minute you're shaking at the sight of an EPE and the next minute you're trying to convince me you're a man in a boy's body! What's your name and just how old are you?"

"My name's Matt Hammond and I'm thirteen."

"And just who in their right mind sends a kid to do a job like this?"

"I've brought many criminals to justice," said Matt. "My last mission was to rid the Republic of Boro of Horando Javeer, and before that I helped the people of Gova defeat the Vorgs."

"Horando Javeer," repeated O'Malley. "I've heard of him."

"Then you'll know what a tyrant he was, and how his gold mine was destroyed."

"And you want me to believe you did that?"

"I did. Sometimes a kid can get into places that adults

can't, and just because I'm thirteen doesn't mean I don't have a brain."

"I'm not trying to be insulting," said O'Malley. "I'm just trying to get to the truth here."

"The truth is that I don't work on my own. I work with two other people—a man named Varl, who's a great scientist and gives me technological advice, and another boy called Targon who's good at strategizing."

O'Malley's face changed. "Okay, *now* we're getting somewhere. You've got partners including an adult. Where are they?"

"On Moji," said Matt with conviction. He just hoped he was right. After all, where else could they be?

"And who do you work for?"

"I can't tell you that, just as you can't tell me who you work for," said Matt, deciding that a secretive answer would fit best with his story.

O'Malley scratched his head and sighed. "Okay, okay," he said. "I'm convinced that you're not playing a game trying to stay onboard the *Dreamseeker*. The question is, where do we go from here? I can't afford to have you messing up my plans."

"My agency sends me coded messages containing valuable information via my computer. I'm willing to share those with you."

"Your computer? You mean *that* old thing?"

"Don't be fooled by the size," said Matt opening up his laptop. "This thing may be much bigger than your neat little gadgets but you don't have anything like it."

"What frequency does it use?"

"No wires and no wireless transmitter either."

O'Malley looked stunned. "How does it work, then?"

"I'm not permitted to say," said Matt, enjoying his secrecy. "But it works well. How do you think I found you?"

"*You* found *me*?" said O'Malley. "I thought it was the other way around!"

Matt gave him a cheeky grin. "That's what I wanted you to think!"

O'Malley laughed. "Okay, kid."

"So who's the other infiltrator?" said Matt.

"And what makes you think that I'm not working on my own?"

Matt pulled up the rhyme. "See, this coded message says *their shields* and refers to *infiltrators* not infiltrator."

"But you don't know who," whispered O'Malley with a smile that said he had one over on Matt.

Matt thought quickly. His gut instinct told him it was the only other discontented individual he'd come across onboard—one who'd actually been pleasant to him. "It's Bart."

O'Malley's smile disappeared. He shook his head. "Wow! You've been busy in the last twenty-four hours. I'm impressed."

"Good," said Matt. He held out his hand. "It'll be a pleasure working with you, Mr. O'Malley."

O'Malley shook his hand. "I never thought a kid could teach me anything in this job. I guess I was wrong.

Sounds as though you'll make my job a lot easier from now on."

Matt smiled at him confidently, but his insides felt like curdling milk. So far so good. But would he be able to stay one step ahead of Conan O'Malley? And would O'Malley trust him enough to share information—particularly if Matt wanted to get off the *Dreamseeker*? He had to get to the Island of Moji and find Varl and Targon if he wanted to win the final level of his game.

Chapter 11

Varl's mouth felt like sandpaper, dry and dusty. His throat was parched and it was hard to swallow. The sight of the water jug on the dresser killed him. Surely someone would check on him soon. This seemed such cruel treatment. He lay on the bed watching the curtains flap in the breeze, occasionally snatching at his wrist restraints in anger and frustration.

The door hinges creaked, but he couldn't raise his head high enough to see who had entered the room.

"Whoever you are, could I please have some water?" he asked, his voice husky.

A petite dark-skinned lady walked over to his bed and bent over him. Her long beaded earrings swung as she moved. "I'll get you some," she said in a curt manner.

He watched her pour water from the jug into a cracked glass. She lifted his head and put the glass to his mouth. The water tasted so good, but even though he drank slowly, most of it slopped over the edge and ran down his chin, soaking his undershirt.

"Why am I tied to the bed?"

"Because we'll be handing you over to the authorities once you are well enough to leave here," she answered.

"The authorities?" said Varl, choking on the water. "What authorities?"

She dabbed his mouth with a small towel. "The federal agents on the mainland."

"But why?"

"Because the people of Moji have had enough of you pirates."

Varl gasped. "Pirates? You think *I'm* a pirate, ma'am? Do I look like a pirate? What could possibly give you that idea?"

"Jarro found you at Balamachu. The tomb gate was open and your shipmates were inside."

"I'm sorry, ma'am, but you're making a dreadful mistake. I don't know anything about a tomb and I don't have shipmates."

"Well, that's for the authorities to decide."

Varl's head was pounding. He groaned.

"You're lucky that Jarro found you when he did. You nearly died from that fall. He could have just left you there to rot. But he's too decent a man."

"Fall?" said Varl. "I had a fall?"

"Your head was split wide open, but I stitched you up. I gave you Arnica to minimize the bruising and Aconite for shock—and a lot of painkillers too."

Varl remembered the jab of the needle. "Thanks," he muttered, trying to recall everything else that had happened.

"It's best you rest your head," she said quietly. "I'll be out back with the chickens. I'll bring you some breakfast later."

The door closed, leaving Varl looking at the curtains once again. He knew his name and he knew that he lived in Zaul, but what was he doing here—a place called Moji? Then it all came flooding back—Targon . . . pirates . . . the pyramid . . . being pushed down the steps of Balamachu. How could he convince these people that he wasn't one of the pirates? And what had happened to Targon?

* * * * *

Targon shoved his hands in his pockets. His misery was like a lead weight. What now? The tomb was empty, Varl was nowhere to be found and he certainly wasn't in any mood to visit Devil's Cove with Gabriela.

"Cheer up," she said as they walked back along the coastal path. "We'll find your friend."

"But how?" asked Targon. "You say the other tombs aren't even worth visiting, and I don't want to wait and see if your father has any news tonight. Varl could be dead by then."

"Well, there's one thing we could try."

"What's that?"

"We could go and see Old Peg on the way to Devil's Cove."

"Old Peg?"

"She's a very old lady who lives in Cala de la

Tortuga."

"Cala de la Tortuga?"

"Turtle Cove," translated Gabriela.

"So how could she help?"

"They say she can tell you anything you want to know—that the spirits talk to her."

"The spirits?" he groaned. "I thought you were joking when you said that you wouldn't let your father set the spirits on me."

"I didn't say I believed in such things. But I do know several people who swear that Old Peg has helped them. Besides, you believe in spirits—you said that you saw the spirit of Queen Elena at Balamachu."

Targon sighed. "Honestly, I don't know what to believe! I'm so confused right now. One minute I remember seeing her spirit, and the next I'm not sure. What if I fell and just imagined the whole thing?"

"You were very certain about what had happened when I found you yesterday," said Gabriela. "Besides, wouldn't you have some cuts and bruises if you had fallen?"

"Thanks for being so positive," said Targon. "And you're right. I'm just very tired and miserable without my friends."

"So shall we go to see Old Peg?"

"It's worth trying. Anything's worth trying—even if it involves talking to spirits," said Targon.

Gabriela chatted all the way along the beach path, telling him about the island and her people. Targon wondered if she ever ran out of things to say. But he wasn't really complaining. He enjoyed her bright personality and he knew that she was deliberately trying to distract him.

The village of Cala de la Tortuga was very different from Pueblo Verde where Gabriela lived—the streets were unpaved and the houses were nothing more than shacks constructed from scrap pieces of wood. The roofs were made from palm fronds and the windows were open holes. Now Targon understood what Gabriela had meant when she'd said that Moji was very primitive compared to other parts of the world. Pueblo Verde had pleasantly surprised him. This village, on the other hand, belonged back in the Stone Age.

Old Peg was sat in a rocking chair on her front porch, humming a melancholy tune. As they walked up the path, she hobbled to her feet. She was no more than five feet tall and bent heavily over. Targon thought she must be over a hundred years old.

"Come in, come in!" she croaked, ushering them into her one-roomed house. She smoothed her silver hair that was tied roughly back. "I don't have anything to offer you to eat. I don't get many visitors."

"That's okay, Old Peg," said Gabriela. "We've come to ask for your help and we'll pay you well."

Old Peg's face lit up when Gabriela produced a wad of bills from her back pocket and handed them to her. She smiled, her weather-beaten face creasing into deep lines. "What can Old Peg do for you?" she said, quickly stuffing the cash into her apron pocket.

"I need to find a friend of mine," said Targon. "His name is Varl."

Old Peg took his hand and led him to a small table in the center of the room. She sat at the end of the table, smoothed out the colored cloth, and straightened a pad of paper and a pencil in the middle. "Sit down next to me, boy," she ordered, taking hold of his hand again. "And you, girl, sit down on the other side of me."

Gabriela pulled out the chair opposite Targon.

Old Peg rubbed her index finger down the back of Targon's hand. He shivered—her hands were thin and bony, the fingers bent with arthritis, and her skin seemed transparent.

"It is an elderly man you are looking for—though he's a young man compared to me." She laughed, breaking into a cough.

"How did you know that?" asked Targon.

"Old Peg knows a lot of things," she answered. "Your friend had an accident and you're very worried about him."

Targon looked across the table at Gabriela in total disbelief.

"I told you she was good," said Gabriela.

Old Peg closed her eyes and muttered in Spanish. She was holding Targon's hand so tightly that he winced.

"The spirits are sending me a message. Girl, write it down," Old Peg ordered.

Targon looked around the room. He couldn't see any

spirits.

Gabriela grabbed the pad and pencil.

"There are five words with four letters in each, though I cannot say what they are. The spirits tell me that you have been to all of these places."

Gabriela was writing fast. Targon was thinking hard.

"You must take the last of the first, the second of the second, the third of the third, the third of the fourth, and find it on the last."

"What does that mean?" asked Targon.

"Wait! There's more—a second set of instructions!" said Old Peg. "Next you need to take the last of the first, the second of the second, the last of the third, the third of the fourth, and find it on the last."

"I don't have any idea what that means," said Targon, as Old Peg opened her eyes again.

"Girl, did you get that down?"

Gabriela nodded.

"Well, you'd better get to work," said Old Peg, getting up from the table. "I'll get us some water."

"What five places have you been that have four letters?" asked Gabriela.

"That's easy," said Targon. "Zaul, Karn, Gova, Javeer, and of course, Moji."

"Javeer can't be right," said Gabriela, chewing the end of the pencil. "It has six letters."

Targon's cheeks flushed. He would have to work on his spelling as well as his reading. "But those *are* the only places I've been."

"Are you *sure* Javeer is right?"

Targon thought hard for a moment. "Boro!" he shouted, suddenly remembering Level 4 of Matt's computer game. "Javeer used to be called Boro!"

"I don't really understand what you mean," said Gabriela, "but that's fine by me. I'll write down Boro."

"So what do you think the rest means?" asked Targon.

"Work with the letters," said Old Peg from the far side of the room. "What was the first place you mentioned, boy?"

"Zaul," said Targon.

"Girl, what did the first instruction say?"

"Take the last of the first," said Gabriela.

Old Peg came back to the table and put a glass of water in front of each of them. "The last letter of the first word is L."

"Oh, now I get it," said Targon.

Gabriela was scribbling away. "This should take no time. The second of the second is the letter A, the third of the third is the letter V, and the third of the fourth is the letter R. Then it says to find it on the last—which is the word Moji."

"That doesn't make any sense," said Targon.

"Play with the letters," said Old Peg.

"L,A,V and R," said Targon. "If you change them around that spells Varl!"

"And we should find him on Moji," said Gabriela.

Targon exhaled heavily. "Well, that doesn't tell us

anything that we don't already know."

"Young people today don't have any patience," snapped Old Peg. "Try the second part."

"Okay," said Gabriela. "If we follow the second set of instructions, we get the letters L,A,A and R, and the last sentence is the same again, meaning Moji."

"Great," said Targon. "That was a waste of time."

"You just don't have any faith, do you, boy?" said Peg.

"You know what it means, then?" asked Targon.

Old Peg grinned. "But of course. The spirits have never let me down."

Especially when there's money involved, thought Targon skeptically. After all, he hadn't *seen* any spirits in the room. This was nothing like what he had experienced at Balamachu. And so far the spirits had only told Old Peg what he'd also told her. He'd said Varl's name right at the beginning and it was obvious that Varl was on Moji. Besides, Old Peg could easily have guessed that Varl had had an accident because Targon was so worried about him.

"Those letters spell Lara," said Old Peg. "There's only one Lara on Moji and everyone's heard of her."

"Lara Santa-Maria," said Gabriela. "She's a healer, isn't she?"

"What's a healer?" asked Targon.

"Lara heals people using natural remedies as well as modern drugs," Old Peg explained. "If your friend Varl was injured, I guarantee she'll have fixed him up good and proper by now. He'll be fine."

"Where do we find her?" asked Targon, getting up to leave.

"Your skepticism seems to have suddenly disappeared now that you have a new direction, boy," Old Peg grumbled. "Suddenly you believe in the power of the spirits."

"If they're right, I'll be a believer forever," said Targon.

Old Peg took his hand and whispered, "Go to the other end of Cala de la Tortuga and you will see a cottage in a clearing. Lara lives there."

* * * * *

"Any chance you can get me something to eat?" Matt asked O'Malley. "I don't want to risk walking around the *Dreamseeker* any more than I have to, and I can't think of a plan on an empty stomach."

O'Malley got to his feet. "I'm sure I can manage that, since I'm going to the kitchen anyway. I trust you'll be here when I get back."

"Like I've got somewhere to go in a hurry," Matt laughed.

O'Malley smiled. "Okay, I'll leave you thinking. You shouldn't be bothered back here—everyone's gone for breakfast."

When the door closed Matt opened his computer once more, glad of the opportunity to pull up his game.

"I need to find out how to locate the Keepers," he

muttered. "I can't deactivate them if I don't know how to find them."

He found the menu and scrolled down the options to Number 9, *The Keeper.*

Once again the *Dreamseeker* appeared on the screen, battling the raging seas. The words to the rhyme materialized in cursive writing, superimposed over the picture.

Find two Keepers if you can
Machine or image, not the man
One on land and one at sea
Help to start the mutiny.
Deactivate may be the game
But destroy will do the same
Careful not to take a life
Let modern justice solve the strife

Matt focused on the individual words and read the rhyme a second, and then a third time. He had so much information swimming around in his brain that he didn't know what he should deal with first. He had been right. There *were* two Keepers once again—one at sea and one on land. He wondered what they were, and how he could be expected to coordinate an attack on both. The rhyme was also telling him that this time there were two groups of people to help him. He figured he had now found the mutineers at sea. But the second group, the islanders, were on Moji and he had yet to find them. Perhaps Varl and Targon would know.

O'Malley arrived back carrying a plate piled high with bacon, sausages and toast. Matt's mouth watered. He put the computer on the floor at his feet. The rhyme could wait until he had eaten.

"Did you find out anything new?" asked O'Malley, his mouth full.

Matt munched his way through a sausage before answering. "Lots," he said.

"Like what?"

"I just received a new coded message from headquarters," Matt lied.

"You'll share the information, I hope."

"Sure, you can read it." Matt licked his greasy fingers and slid his laptop across the floor.

O'Malley put down the plate and picked up the computer. He read the rhyme silently and grunted. "And you can decipher the code that's embedded in this?"

"It's not so much deciphering as understanding. It takes thought, but I always get there."

"So what's a Keeper?"

Fortunately Matt had anticipated that this would be one of O'Malley's first questions. "The Keeper is the tool by which Captain Persivius Scarr will achieve his goals. My headquarters are now telling me that there are two Keepers."

"Yeah, I get that—one on land and one at sea."

"I have to deactivate or destroy them both in order to bring down Scarr—"

"—Without killing any civilians in the process,"

O'Malley cut in.

Matt smiled. This was going well. "You got it," he said.

"I don't know which government you're working for, and to be honest, I don't really care," said O'Malley. "What *is* important is that we're working to achieve the same thing." He ran his hands through his thick hair and exhaled noisily. "Persivius Scarr—for years I've been trying to gather enough evidence to put him away. I'm so close. But he'll be able to blow up much more than a cruise ship if we don't stop him soon. The man's got a small arsenal somewhere on Moji. Rumor has it that he's even developed a new guided missile called a CGP."

"CGP?"

"Counter-gravity projectile."

"And you've got to find the arsenal before he uses it," said Matt.

"Now *you've* got it," said O'Malley.

Chapter 12

Targon stood outside the little cottage in the clearing. He and Gabriela were a long way from any other house in Cala de la Tortuga. The house was bigger than Old Peg's—perhaps two rooms instead of one—but just as run down. The steps up to the front porch were rotting and the roof looked as though it wouldn't survive the next thunderstorm. The bright green curtains flapping in the windows were all that gave the wooden structure any color.

"Lara Santa-Maria, please be here," muttered Targon as he knocked on the door. His heart raced. Was Varl here too?

They waited. There was no sound from within and no one came to the door.

"She doesn't seem to be home," said Gabriela. "Try again."

Targon sighed. Surely they hadn't come all this way for nothing. Why had he let his hopes get so high? He knew he shouldn't have believed Old Peg. She had just wanted money.

"She might be in her garden. Let's walk around back," said Gabriela.

Targon followed her around the corner of the shack

and past an open window. He peeked inside. His heart stopped.

"Varl! It's Varl!" he gasped. "He's lying on the bed!"

"Targon?" Varl groaned.

Targon could hardly contain his excitement. "Varl's alive! Look, Gabriela!"

"We've found him! I'm so happy for you," Gabriela said, coming back to peer through the window.

"Targon, is that you, my boy?" Varl whispered.

"Varl, you're alive! I can't believe it!"

"Shh! Keep your voice down," said Varl.

It was then that Targon saw the fear in Varl's eyes. "Are you okay?" he whispered back.

"My wrists and legs are tied to the bed!"

"They are? Why?"

"Just climb through the window and untie me! Hurry! She'll be back at any time. I'll explain later."

Targon was about to hoist himself up when he heard the door hinges creak. Just as someone walked into the room, he ducked under the windowsill and pulled Gabriela down next to him.

"Hungry, Varl?" he heard a woman ask.

"Yes, but I don't see how I can eat when you've tied me to this bed."

"I'll cut one hand loose and help you sit up. But don't try anything. Jarro will be back at any moment."

"Honestly, ma'am, I'm not a pirate. I don't know anything about any tomb and I certainly won't do you any harm," said Varl, loudly and clearly.

Targon looked at Gabriela. They had to get him out of there!

"There you go. You should be able to eat now."

"Thank you," said Varl.

"I hear Jarro's truck. I'll be back in a minute. I'll change that bandage on your head when you're done."

When Targon heard the door close, he leaped to his feet and threw himself through the open window, landing awkwardly on the floor. "Ouch!" He scrambled to his feet and hobbled across the room.

Gabriela came in after him. "What kind of mad move was that?" she asked.

"Are you okay, my boy?" asked Varl.

"I'm fine. Let's just worry about you," said Targon, leaning over the bed.

"My head is still pounding, but if you can untie me, I might be able to climb on something and get out through the window," said Varl.

Targon looked around the room. "What did she cut the rope with?"

"She had a knife," said Varl. "I guess she took it away with her."

"Zang it!" said Targon. "We'll have to undo the knots." He worked on the rope tied to Varl's left wrist while Gabriela started on the ropes around his feet.

"This knot is too tight," said Gabriela. "I'm not getting anywhere."

"I've got this one," said Targon, pulling off the rope.

Varl rubbed his wrists. "That feels better."

Targon raced to the foot of the bed and began loosening the rope tied to Varl's right foot.

"Success!" Gabriela finally announced.

"Yes!" said Targon. "I've got this one too."

They helped Varl to his feet and walked him to the window.

Varl grabbed the edge of the window for support. "I don't know how I'm going to do this," he groaned. "Even if you drag the bed over to the window for me to stand on, I'll never make it down the other side."

"You're darn right, you won't!" growled a deep voice at the door. "Get away from the window!"

Targon swung around to see a tall bearded black man standing in the doorway wielding a bread knife. It had to be Jarro. He was well built with massive shoulders and muscular arms. Targon drew in a deep breath. He and Gabriela would be no match for him.

A small dark-skinned woman came in and stood next to him. *Lara*, thought Targon.

"Lara Santa-Maria, Old Peg sent us here to see you," pleaded Targon. "She'll tell you that you've made a big mistake."

The woman seemed surprised that Targon had used her name. "And how have we made a mistake?" she asked.

Jarro stepped closer and stuck out the knife defensively.

"You must be Jarro," said Targon. He looked into the man's gentle eyes and added, "I can see that you're not the kind of man who would hurt innocent people, especially kids."

Jarro lowered the knife. "Okay, kid. I'll give you five minutes to explain what you're doing here and why you're releasing our prisoner."

"Varl is my friend. He's a scientist and we're here on vacation from Zaul."

"So what were you doing at Balamachu, and more importantly, why were you down in the tomb?" Jarro asked.

"We found Balamachu by accident when we were exploring the area. I climbed the pyramid because I'd been learning about ancient tombs. Varl stayed at the bottom because of his bad knees."

"So how did he end up at the bottom of the steps inside the pyramid?" asked Lara.

"I can answer that. I'm beginning to remember now," said Varl, touching the bandage on the back of his head. He winced with the pain. "I was waiting for Targon when two pirates held me at gunpoint and forced me to climb the pyramid. They had some booty to hide. I remember that I was having trouble with the steps going down inside the pyramid and I refused to go any farther."

"They pushed Varl down the steps," said Targon. "I was hiding in the shadows just outside the tomb gate and I saw everything. I thought he was dead. I was terrified."

Jarro scratched his beard. "So where were you when I found Varl and carried him out of there?"

Targon hesitated, wondering how much he could

honestly admit. "I don't know if you'll believe me."

"Try me," said Jarro. "I've listened so far, haven't I?"

Targon recounted how he had learned the password from the two pirates and entered the tomb.

"So you're telling me that it was you I saw inside the tomb and not pirates when I snuck down the steps," said Jarro.

"You didn't tell *me* that part!" Gabriela shrieked. "And why didn't you tell my father that the pirates were hiding booty in our tomb?"

Targon stared at his feet. This would hurt her terribly, but he had to say it. "Because I think your father already knows that."

"Her father?" said Jarro. "Who's her father?"

"Mowann Kimile," replied Targon.

Jarro suddenly relaxed his threatening stance. "I've believed for a long time that our mayor was involved with the pirates."

"It's not true!" shouted Gabriela. "It's all lies! You're making the whole thing up. Targon, how could you turn on my family after I helped you? We've just been to the tomb. I shone the flashlight through the gate. There was nothing there!"

"Well, there was certainly something there yesterday afternoon," said Jarro. "As I came down the steps I could see that the lights were on in the tomb. The gate was wide open and I could see money and gold from where I was standing."

"What a relief," said Targon. "At least I now know I

really did see all of that."

"I didn't want to risk a confrontation as I was unarmed and didn't know how many pirates were inside the tomb," continued Jarro. "I just saw shadows moving. I was going to run and get the police when I saw Varl. I assumed that he was one of the pirates and had slipped on the worn out steps. I'm not a man who would leave anyone to die, and so I decided to bring him to Lara. That way I also had one of the pirates to turn over to the authorities."

Varl was holding onto the windowsill for support. "Thank you for saving my life," he said in a raspy voice.

"Varl, you're still very weak. Sit back down on the bed," said Lara softly.

Jarro nodded and put the knife down on the cupboard next to the door. "And I promise we won't tie you up again."

"None of you are making any sense!" Gabriela shouted. "Why would the pirate booty be there yesterday and not today?"

"I think that your father had everything moved out of Balamachu last night after he realized that it might soon be discovered," said Targon. "That's what all of those late night calls were about."

"No! How can you say that? My father was helping you find Varl. He wants the pirates off Moji like everyone else. He's said so many times. He wouldn't do anything to help them hide their booty!"

"I'm sorry, Miss Kimile, but there are a lot of people

on Moji who believe that your father and other island officials *are* making deals with the pirates for their own profit."

"Making deals with the pirates? How dare you accuse him of that! I won't hear any more!" Gabriela ran from the room crying, "You're wrong! You're all wrong!"

"I'd better go after her," said Targon. He felt sick to his stomach for hurting her.

Jarro shook his head. "I'd leave her for a while. She'll calm down and think about everything you've said."

"Or go running straight to her father," said Lara. "And he'll have us all locked up in order to protect himself!"

* * * * *

Two Keepers, thought Matt as he finished eating the last piece of bacon. The rhyme had been specific—a machine or an image, but not a man. In the first four levels of his game the Keeper had been a controlling factor of the level, often connected to a computer and usually linked to a tyrant. He thought about the glistening control room on the raised platform at the other end of the hold. It was certainly the most high-tech thing he'd seen onboard the *Dreamseeker*. What exactly did it control? Would he be able to get a closer look?

"How much do you know about the control room in the hold?" asked Matt.

"What? You mean the computers on the platform out there?"

Matt nodded.

"They can completely control the mini-subs and airlocks when needed," said O'Malley. "They also control the torpedoes onboard the *Dreamseeker* and send the coded messages to the cruise ships."

"Coded messages?"

"Scarr has set up a system to send specific instructions to the cruise ship captains before the mini-subs pull up alongside to raid the ships. Information about where the crew should be standing, where the pirates are coming aboard, and so on. If the captain of the cruise ship doesn't comply, the ship will be sunk with torpedoes. The cruise ships know the code that is embedded in the message to identify that it is a real attack and not a hoax. Scarr has already blown one magnificent ship out of the water and severely damaged another. This message cannot be traced back to the *Dreamseeker* and neither can the torpedoes."

"Wow!" said Matt. "It sounds pretty sophisticated. So the captains do what they're told out of fear for their passengers and their ships, but they have no idea where the attacks are launched from."

"Exactly. During a raid, life onboard the cruise ship continues pretty much as normal. Since the pirates only take money and jewelry from the ship's safe and from a few wealthy passengers onboard, the majority of the passengers never know that a raid has taken place."

"So the captains just comply and the raiders take what they want."

"But these attacks are becoming more frequent and word is getting out. If we don't put a stop to this soon, it will ruin the cruise industry."

"And meanwhile, Scarr is getting really rich," added Matt.

"As I told you earlier, we think there's much more to it than that," said O'Malley. "It is believed that Persivius Scarr is part of a terrorist organization. My government is seriously worried that he has developed a new missile that he has stockpiled somewhere on Moji. The consequences could be dire! My mission is to get to the bottom of his operation, find out what is happening to the booty that pays for the weapons, where the weapons are hidden, and also who is helping him on land. Until I know all that, I have to stay undercover. Otherwise we would have stopped his pirate escapades long ago."

Matt remembered the lines from the second rhyme.

Scarr's raids are not for wealth or fame
His booty is for a dangerous game
But many governments are aware
Against attack they must prepare

He felt elated. Conan O'Malley's revelations had just filled in a lot of the blanks.

"I've got to get out of this jumpsuit and back into costume," said O'Malley. "We've got another round of visitors due onboard the *Dreamseeker* at two."

"And you have to help with the tour?" said Matt.

"The *Dreamseeker*'s crew is currently only sixty

men."

"It's hard to believe that this ship once carried two hundred men."

"I know—it seems cramped with sixty. Every member of the crew is expected to participate in the tour for two reasons. It takes a lot of hands to raise and lower the sails, heave up the jolly boat and operate the capstan. But more important, there are often tour inspectors and officials from Moji who come aboard with a tour. Scarr wants them to believe that all sixty men he employs are involved with his so-called 17th Century Pirate Adventures. He doesn't want any suspicion that something else might be going on."

"What about the huge rocket launcher I saw on deck last night? Or, at least I presume that's what was under that plastic tarp."

"Observant of you," said O'Malley. "The rocket launcher is stored beneath the Forecastle. It is only for emergency protection of this ship and raised only just before a raid. Once the men are all back safely, it is quickly lowered again."

"I haven't seen the torpedo launchers."

O'Malley smiled. "Only seen by a privileged few. The launch room is located right in the bow below the control room."

"It's all very well thought out, for sure," said Matt.

"I'll have to change my clothing again after the tour, as I'm going ashore with the booty at dusk. It'll be my first chance to see where it's hidden."

"Can you get me on the jolly boat too?" asked Matt eagerly. "I need to meet up with the rest of my team and locate the second Keeper."

"I'll do my best, but it's not a very big boat, as you know, and Hawkeye handpicks the shore crew. That was a big raid last night so there's already five of us going."

"I've got a better idea," said Matt. "I'll go ashore with the tourists in the motorboat this afternoon and I'll get back onboard during the next tour tomorrow."

"Sounds like a good plan. Once you're back onboard, I'll find a way to get you down here."

"Only one problem," said Matt. "I don't have any regular clothing to blend in with the tourists."

"What about what you were wearing yesterday?" asked O'Malley.

Matt broke into a cold sweat. He couldn't tell O'Malley the truth—that the clothes came from Level 4 of his computer game and the mines of Horando Javeer. "What? That old red top and baggy pants?" he snorted. "Forget that! I'd stand out like a sore thumb. Scarr and Hawkeye would recognize me instantly and wonder what I'd been doing onboard the *Dreamseeker* for the last twenty-four hours."

"Mmm," said O'Malley. "Good point. But there's still no problem. Scarr insists that we dress in period costume for the tourists, but everyone onboard has a personal locker with clothing for shore leave. There are a couple of cabin boys that are about your size. I'll take a look in their lockers and see if I can find something to fit you."

Matt watched O'Malley leave. With any luck in another few hours he'd be on Moji with Varl and Targon. How he hated the waiting game. One thing was for sure—Conan O'Malley was going to be a very useful ally.

Chapter 13

"So are we free to go?" asked Varl, looking uncomfortably at his captors.

Jarro nodded. "You are—since it now seems that we are on the same side."

Lara handed Varl a glass of water. "I'm sorry that we held you prisoner. I feel really badly."

"It's okay," said Varl. "I understand your reasoning, even if it was an unpleasant experience. However, I'm truly grateful to you both for saving my life."

"But Jarro, what were you doing at Balamachu?" asked Targon. "Gabriela told me that Balamachu is on private property and hardly anyone ever goes there."

"I'm very lucky that you were there," added Varl.

"Actually, it wasn't a matter of luck," said Jarro. "I was at Balamachu on purpose."

"How so?" asked Varl.

"I work for the security department of the port authority based at Bahia Del Tigre. We're losing a lot of the cruise trade because of the pirate problem. Because the cruise companies are diverting their ships to other areas, our shopkeepers and tour companies are losing a lot of money. Moji's economy cannot survive without the tourist money. So, I'm trying to do something about it."

"You're saying that pirates are attacking cruise ships? They're huge things, aren't they?" asked Varl.

Jarro nodded. "Most of them are 90,000 tons and carry at least 2,000 passengers."

Varl shook his head in disbelief. "The pirates must have fast, well-armed boats to bring a cruise ship to a stop."

"The problem is far bigger than that," said Jarro. "Their method is clever and untraceable. They send coded messages to the captain to say an attack is underway, and then pull up next to the cruise ship in small craft that are a cross between a boat and a submarine. Money and jewelry is taken from the ship safe and from specific passengers."

"Which would suggest that someone on the mainland is providing inside knowledge about who is onboard each cruise ship," said Varl.

"Exactly," said Jarro. "And the pirates are on and off the cruise ships within fifteen minutes. They're gone before any police or armed forces can get there, and they have some kind of high-tech system that prevents the coast guard from tracking their subs."

"Zang it!" said Targon. "That's incredible!"

"It does seem both clever and highly organized," said Varl. "So why don't the captains refuse to stop their ships? How much damage can small arms from a tiny sub cause to a 90,000-ton ship?"

"A lot," said Jarro. "First, there are usually two subs, both fitted with rocket launchers. They put a huge hole in the side of one ship when the crew tried to arrest the pirates coming aboard."

"Really," said Varl.

"But that's not the worst of it," continued Jarro. "They blew one cruise ship out of the water for not stopping and letting them onboard. Many people died. The pirating was covered up by local governments as terrorist activity."

Varl shook his head in disbelief. "All this from a tiny sub?"

Jarro snorted. "No, this is clever. They used torpedoes that are locked onto the cruise ship when the raid begins from some unknown location. The captains are threatened that the torpedoes will be fired if there are any problems during the raid. So far no one has been able to work out where exactly the torpedoes are controlled from. I'm determined to find it."

"We'd like to help you," said Varl.

Lara laughed. "I don't think you're in any fit state!"

"I'll be fit again in no time. In fact, I'm already feeling much better." Varl stood up to prove his point.

"Besides, you're on vacation," said Jarro.

"It'll make our vacation much more fun," said Targon. "And I think we can help you."

"We know what ship those pirates at Balamachu came from," said Varl.

Jarro looked surprised. "You do?"

"The *Dreamseeker*," said Targon.

Jarro roared with laughter. "I think you're confusing fake pirates with real ones."

Varl frowned. "What do you mean?"

"The *Dreamseeker* is an old 17th-century three-masted square-rigger that has been set up as a tourist attraction. It sails between Moji and other islands in the area giving daily tours onboard. The crew dress up like pirates and even give demonstrations of walking the plank. It's just a lot of fun that brings in money and trade on the island. How do you think that an old ship like that could attack a cruise ship?"

"I don't know," said Varl. "But I think that you have to consider the possibility that some of its crew are involved in pirating in some way."

"Just think about it," said Targon more forcefully. "Why were two of the *Dreamseeker*'s crew at Balamachu hiding booty? Why was 'Dreamseeker' the code that opened the tomb? And why are they holding our friend, Matt, as a prisoner onboard the *Dreamseeker*?"

Jarro raised his eyebrows. "Your friend Matt?"

"We got separated yesterday," said Targon.

Varl walked over to the window and stretched. "The reason we were following the pirates in the first place is because we heard them talking about holding Matt onboard."

"Okay," said Jarro. "Perhaps the *Dreamseeker is* worth investigating. How do you fancy taking one of the *Dreamseeker*'s tours this afternoon?"

"You bet!" said Targon.

Varl shook his head. "I think I should stay here. I'm better," he said, "But I don't want to overdo it."

"I'll stay with Varl and make sure that he rests," said Lara. "Then he'll be fit tomorrow."

Jarro looked at his watch. "The tours are at two o'clock. We'd better hurry if we're going to get to Bahia Del Tigre in time."

"I'll pack you some sandwiches to eat on the way," said Lara.

"No time," said Jarro. "We'll pick something up at the port."

"And Targon," said Varl, looking him straight in the eye. "You stay with Jarro. Don't go wandering away from the tour trying to play hero, looking for Matt on your own."

"I promise," said Targon, making a speedy exit.

"We'll be back around five," said Jarro. "Varl, don't worry about the boy. I'll see that he doesn't get up to any mischief."

Varl lay back down on the bed and closed his eyes, but he knew he wouldn't rest. He listened to Jarro's truck driving away at speed. Mischief was not what he was worried about—he knew Targon would do anything to find Matt and that meant Targon could get in trouble. He wouldn't be able to relax until they were back.

* * * * *

Matt gasped when O'Malley came back into the little room dressed in a knotted scarf and woolen stockings. "I hardly recognize you!"

"That's the general idea," O'Malley replied. "Just wait

'til ye 'ear me talk like 'em too."

Matt chuckled. "You're good!"

"I have to be. We're only allowed to lose the accent when we're in the hold, on raids, or going ashore. The rest of the time we have to stay in character. Scarr wants a complete distinction between the 17th century pirate adventure tours and his real pirating operation, so that no one will ever connect the two. The locals just think it's a load of fun and a great draw for the tourists."

"It must be hard to switch back and forth between accents."

"It's not easy," said O'Malley. "I've been known to forget."

"Thanks for finding the shorts and T-shirt for me." Matt held them up against himself. "They'll fit."

"And here's a cap too."

"Great! Thanks!"

"You can thank Bart next time you see him," said O'Malley. "He went through everyone's locker."

Suddenly a shrill siren sounded. Matt covered his ears.

"There's the five-minute warning siren," said O'Malley. "It's 1:55. I've got to get on deck."

"I can't wait to get out of here," shouted Matt above the din. Finally the long blast ended and he lowered his hands.

"Just remember, the hold is locked down while the tourists are onboard, so you'll be here on your own. There'll be a second siren in a minute to tell you that everyone is out of the hold and the hatch has been locked. Then, in just over a ninety minutes, you'll hear a third siren signaling the end of the tour. At that point the hatches to the hold will automatically unlock and you'll have about one minute to get up the steps to Orlop deck before some of the crew will be back down here. Just make sure you change into the shorts and T-shirt first."

"Right," said Matt. "I've got it."

"Then make your way through the sail room to the bow and you'll see the ramp and the motorboat waiting. When the tourists board you should be able to slip into line."

"Thanks," said Matt. "While the tour is going on, I'll use my time down here to look at the computers."

"Good, because I've not been able to get near them," said O'Malley.

"How long does the tour last?"

"Usually about ninety minutes. It starts on Main deck with a short pirate skit and a demonstration of walking the plank. Then the tourists are taken down to Gun deck and through the various sections of Orlop deck. At the end they'll board the boats back to shore."

"Great."

"Must go," said O'Malley. "They'll be looking for me."

Matt shook his hand. "Thanks, O'Malley."

"You're welcome. Good luck to you. If all goes well, I'll see you tomorrow."

The door closed. Matt paced, waiting for the siren and his chance to examine Scarr's computers. He listened at the door and couldn't hear a sound—a good sign. He put his hand on the doorknob. "Wait," he muttered to himself. "Patience."

The second siren sounded, indicating the beginning of lockdown. Matt waited another minute for good measure, and then crept stealthily out of the room, past the lockers and into the huge hold. He stood for a minute absorbing the magnitude of the room, the airlocks and the control platform. Until now he'd been whisked through the area and had not had a chance to really look at the equipment. Much as he detested Persivius Scarr, he had to admire his ingenious operation.

The room seemed spooky with no one else there. Matt walked carefully around the edge of the airlocks and over to the platform in the bow. The center of operations seemed much bigger now that he was standing directly in front of the platform. He stepped up to get a closer look.

Three curved smoke-gray desks in a semicircle covered the entire width of the platform. Behind the desks at intervals were three enormous computer screens, double the size of the largest TV screen he'd ever seen back home. Two of the screens were turned off, but on the center one was a nautical map of the area. For the first time Matt could see where Moji was in relation to the other small islands nearby. He guessed that the map was used for co-ordinates of the cruise ships during a raid and also to pinpoint the *Dreamseeker*'s location.

At first the computers linked to the screens were not

visible. It was only when Matt sat in one of the chairs that the desktop slid back, revealing a keyboard.

"Sweet!" he muttered as he fingered the keys. At least this time the letters on the keyboard were all in English! But he soon found out that Scarr's computer system was much more advanced than anything he'd previously seen. Hard as he tried, he could not understand the computer language. There would be no way he could break into the system.

"Zang it! Now what?" He was convinced that the control center was one of the two Keepers in Level 5 of his game. "Keeper of the Island," he muttered. This had to be the Keeper of Scarr's piracy operation. It controlled the coded messages sent to the ships, the activation of torpedoes, and the mini-subs and airlock doors. As long as this computer was operating it allowed Scarr to successfully attack cruise ships.

Matt felt suddenly cold. If Scarr could launch torpedoes from this computer system, what would be the betting that he could also launch his new CGP's? Then the whole world would be at Scarr's mercy! But how could Matt deactivate or destroy this Keeper if he couldn't even access the computer system?

Matt kicked the table leg in frustration and immediately regretted it. He massaged his throbbing foot. Losing his self-control would not help the situation. He looked up at the digital clock. The large red numbers showed that an hour had already passed.

Scarr's computer system would have to wait. If Matt

couldn't hack into the system and cause it to malfunction, then he'd have to find another way of destroying the computer. But first, he needed to get back to the room and change into the shorts and T-shirt. He couldn't afford to miss his one-minute window of opportunity to join the tourists heading for Moji.

Chapter 14

"Welcome aboard, me mateys. I be Cap'n Persivius Scarr and this 'ere is me Quartermaster, 'awkeye."

Several tourists in front of Targon laughed and said, "Ooooo, arrrrr," as they shook Scarr's hand and stepped onboard the *Dreamseeker*.

Targon veered away so he wouldn't have to shake the man's hand. It wasn't just Scarr's beady eyes and crooked teeth that made him back away; the man gave off an evil aura, which he felt was more than just part of the pirate act.

Targon followed the other tourists onto the ship. He turned and checked that Jarro was behind, taking note of a locked cupboard door in the bow by the boarding ramp.

The line in front stopped. Everyone gathered round a dark-skinned teenage boy with large gold hoop earrings. He adjusted his headscarf over his tight black curls and said in a loud voice, "I be Skimmy McFinn, and if yer'll come with me, mateys, we'll be startin' our adventure on the Main deck. Should we do battle while ye be onboard, come get yer pistols and a cutlass from 'ere."

There were giggles from some of the girls in the group. Targon decided that he didn't need to check for

Matt in that cupboard!

As they climbed up the steps to Gun deck and finally into the fresh air, he glanced in every direction. But there was no sign of Matt. What had he expected? That Matt would be out swabbing the decks? If Scarr was holding him hostage he'd be locked away somewhere down below.

Jarro touched his arm as they congregated with the others on deck. "Don't worry about your friend," he whispered. "We'll find him if he's here. We can always come back tomorrow."

Targon nodded. That was easy for Jarro to say—Matt wasn't his best friend.

Hawkeye appeared from below. "Alright, me able seamen. 'ow ye all doin' t'day?" He adjusted his eye-patch. "Article number 1, while ye be onboard t'day, no strikin' one another on deck. Every man's quarrels to be ended on shore by sword or pistol!"

The group roared with laughter.

"Article number 2, while ye be onboard t'day, keep yer pistols fit for service, an' any man seen desertin' the ship this afternoon will be punished by death. Do ye all understand?"

Everyone shouted, "Aye," in unison and the group laughed again.

Targon's stomach was clenched tightly. So far he'd had no opportunity to sneak away from the group. He found himself unable to concentrate on the tour.

Scarr arrived on deck.

"Welcome, me landlubbers," he declared. "First, you all will bear witness this afternoon to the punishment of Dead-leg Joe. 'e's about to walk the plank for stealin' the booty and will soon be in Davy Jones's locker."

"Davy Jones's locker? What's that?" asked a small boy.

Scarr grinned, his teeth protruding crookedly. He walked over to the boy and poked him hard in the chest. "That's the place at the bottom of the sea reserved for pirates," he said in a threatening voice. "I suggest you be good for your mom unless you also want to visit Davy Jones's locker."

The boy looked as if he was about to cry. His mother put her arm around him and frowned at Scarr, who shrugged his shoulders and turned back to the rest of the group.

"Get Dead-leg Joe up 'ere," snarled Scarr. "Let's feed 'im to the fish!"

Targon watched carefully. Everyone was focused on Dead-leg Joe and the plank of wood.

The pirates started to chant, "Feed the fish! Feed the fish!"

The tourists joined in, clapping in rhythm. This was the chance Targon had been waiting for! He wormed his way to the back of the group and looked behind. A large group of pirates was getting ready to present a skit in the middle of Main deck while another group was testing ropes. It was now or never.

Targon crept to the hatch and quickly backed down

the steps to Gun deck. With one quick look he knew that Scarr would not be able to hide Matt on this deck. Much as he wanted to stay and look at the cannons, his focus was finding his friend. He looked for another hatch and made his way aft between the cannons.

"Oy! Boy! What yer be doin' down 'ere?"

Targon stopped in his tracks. His heart skipped a beat. He turned to see a fat pirate waddling toward him, his belly rolls jiggling over the top of his pants.

"Zang it!" muttered Targon. That was the end of his search. He felt suddenly drained of energy, worried for his friend and desperately sad that he couldn't get to him.

"Yer the second blond boy this week 'o's been nosin' around where 'e shouldn't."

The *second* blond boy? Targon's mood lifted. "I'm sorry. I was looking for the bathroom."

"Ye be wantin' Main deck. There be a special bathroom for tourists."

"Er, Mr. . . . could you show me where it is?"

"I be Billy Rogers not Mr. anythin'. And ye can find it yerself. It's up by the cap'n's cabin."

So much for trying to get him to talk, thought Targon.

"And don't come down 'ere again without the rest of yer tour," added Rogers. "Or the Cap'n 'll throw ye in the brig like he did the other kid."

"Is he still in the brig?" asked Targon, hopefully.

"Is 'e what?" Billy Rogers grimaced. "Course 'e ain't! 'e went ashore with everyone else!"

"Thanks," mumbled Targon.

As he rejoined the group and listened to the rest of the tour his emotions were in turmoil. It seemed that Jarro had been right after all. The *Dreamseeker* was just a tourist boat. He was happy that Matt was not being held hostage, but where was he?

"You okay?" asked Jarro as they sat in the motorboat for the return journey to Moji.

"I feel miserable," said Targon. "I thought that Varl and I were onto something. I know what we saw at Balamachu *and* I know what we heard. The pirates that stole all that booty were from the *Dreamseeker*. It just doesn't make sense."

Jarro patted him on the knee. "Matt will turn up somewhere on Moji."

"Last one comin' aboard," said Skimmy McFinn to the motorboat crew. As Targon looked up to watch them untie the ropes, he caught sight of a boy in a red cap sitting at the stern of the motorboat.

If only that boy were Matt—he'd be feeling so happy right now. He did a double take. The boy looked like Matt, with his freckled face. He couldn't see all of the boy's hair under the cap, but what he could see was strange. Some of it seemed to be blond like Matt's but some of it looked black! And was that a backpack at his feet? It looked like the one that Matt had carried in Level 4 of his game.

Their eyes met. Targon gulped. It *was* Matt! But Matt wasn't smiling and his eyes showed panic.

Matt raised a finger to his lips. Targon immediately understood and turned away. One of the pirates was standing right behind Matt, holding onto the mooring rope of the motorboat. Would the pirate spot Matt before they pulled away from the *Dreamseeker*?

"Cast off, me mateys," Skimmy McFinn shouted. "Thank ye all for takin' Cap'n Scarr's 17th century pirate adventure."

The operator of the motorboat opened the throttle and they sped away from the *Dreamseeker*.

Targon's heart was bursting with delight. He turned back and waved at his friend excitedly. Matt waved back—he was grinning from ear to ear. At last the three of them would be together. They would all be celebrating tonight!

* * * * *

Matt sat in the old rocking chair on Lara's front porch, exhausted from recounting his tale of fear and discovery. He looked up at the setting sun—it had taken over an hour to tell the whole story, and he hoped he hadn't forgotten any important details.

Varl got to his feet and hugged him again. Targon still wasn't satisfied and wanted more information, even though there was no more to give, and Jarro kept shaking his head in disbelief, repeating, "*Dreamseeker*—who would've guessed?"

Matt finally said, "Enough! I'm starving." He pulled himself off the rocker and helped Varl inside for dinner.

The smell of barbequed chicken filled the small house. Lara had gone to a lot of trouble to provide a nice meal to celebrate his escape. While he tucked into the succulent chicken and ripped off chunks of warm bread, he listened to Targon tell an equally riveting tale.

"Wow!" said Matt, wiping his greasy fingers on his pants. "Seems like you and Varl had an adventure of your own."

"And it's not over yet," said Targon, excitement in his voice.

Jarro laughed. "I think you've done quite enough. You can all get on with enjoying your vacation and leave Scarr to the proper authorities, like I'm now going to do. It seems as though Conan O'Malley is doing a fine job. I'm very relieved that federal agents are involved."

Matt remembered his rhyme. He had to get the islanders to help him in order to win Level 5 of his game. He had a feeling that meeting up with Lara and Jarro was no coincidence.

"Dessert, anyone?" asked Lara, getting up from the table.

Jarro stood and began to carry the dirty plates to the sink.

Matt turned to Varl and Targon and whispered, "Sorry, but we've got to tell them we're not tourists. We need their help for Level 5."

Targon shrugged.

Varl nodded his approval.

Matt waited for Jarro to sit back down and then he

said, "Actually, we're not going to be leaving Scarr to the authorities because we're not really tourists."

Jarro looked at Lara and then back at Matt. "How do you mean?"

"I'm sorry I had to lie to you," said Varl, "but after you tied me to the bed, I wasn't sure who you were, or if I could trust you."

Jarro looked alarmed. He put down his spoon and said, "Where's this all leading? Who *are* you all?"

Matt continued with the lie. "We're undercover agents working with Conan O'Malley. Our government is very concerned about the threat of Persivius Scarr's new weapons."

Lara had turned white. "What government is that?"

"I'm sorry, but we're not at liberty to say," said Varl. "Let's just say that our government is one that is friendly to Moji and the other islands around here. I'm sure you understand that we are already divulging privileged information here and can only tell you so much."

"You three? An old man and two boys—undercover agents?" Jarro snorted.

"And it's a good cover," said Matt. "We had you fooled." He decided that there was only one thing to do. He got up and fetched his backpack. "This device sends me coded messages from our government," he said, pulling out his computer and booting it up. "One of the messages told us to find you both."

Lara and Jarro were both wide-eyed and silent.

"They contact us daily in the form of rhymes," said

Matt. "We asked for more information about Scarr's weapons. Let's see what they've sent back to us."

"Number 7?" asked Targon.

"Exactly," said Matt, amazed that Targon had memorized the game menu.

Jarro suddenly got to his feet and backed away from the table. "Just hold on!" he shouted, his voice cracking. "Don't touch your keyboard! How do I know it isn't some sort of weapon?"

Matt was taken aback by his outburst. He looked at Varl for help.

"Jarro, I assure you that we're not going to harm you or Lara in any way," said Varl in a quiet, calm voice. "Our government needs your help. Your island needs your help—as does Conan O'Malley. We're all on the same side and we all need to pull together to rid the world of Persivius Scarr, once and for all."

"I'm honestly just going to pull up the latest message from my government on my computer and with any luck you can help us decipher it," said Matt. He looked at Jarro with pleading eyes, his hand poised over the computer keyboard.

There was stony silence. Jarro seemed deep in thought. Finally, his mouth set and tight-lipped, he sat back down. "Okay. I don't see what choice we have. We'll have to trust you. But I want to see everything you do."

"Okay," said Matt. He swiveled the screen toward Jarro, and Varl and Targon stood behind looking over his shoulder. He pressed Number 7, *Weapons*, on the menu and waited for the picture and rhymes.

> Cutlass and pistol for days gone by
> In modern times look to the sky
> CGP's kill so many more
> Heavy and not easy to store
> The second Keeper will protect
> Use the password to deflect
> Deactivate the Keeper to remove
> Or you'll find the Keeper rules.

"I know what it means. I've seen the CGP's!" Targon screamed.

"You have?" said Jarro.

"Sure. They were in the tomb at Balamachu—stacked against the back wall. I didn't know what the crates were, or what CGP meant. But when Gabriela and I went back this morning, the tomb had been cleared and the crates were gone, along with the rest of the booty."

On the screen appeared a picture of a heavy metal box with the letters CGP stamped in red on the side.

"There! That's what the crates looked like!" said Targon.

"What exactly is a CGP?" asked Varl.

"I've no idea," said Jarro.

"Counter-gravity projectile," said Matt, pulling up a labeled picture on his computer. "Conan O'Malley told me about them."

The CGP rotated 360 degrees on the screen.

"Looks just like a rocket with a huge nose cone," said Targon.

"It is," said Matt. "But it says here that when a CGP is activated it eliminates gravity in a quarter-mile radius. Anything not built into solid rock is accelerated upwards and will end up thousands of feet above the Earth. Then, when the effect of the CGP diminishes a few seconds later, everything that was propelled upward plummets back to Earth."

"Zang it!" said Targon.

"Unbelievable!" said Varl. "But that's technology for you, my boy."

"It's no wonder that Conan O'Malley was sent to track Scarr," said Jarro. "And I thought the pirating off our shores was just about getting rich. This is really something to worry about. Can you imagine what these things could do to a country?"

"We have to find these CGP's and destroy them," said Matt.

"Unfortunately that's not an option for us," said Varl. He pointed to the screen. "If you read the specs, you'll see that the weapons are powered by highly radioactive nuclear material. Deactivation would have to be done in a controlled environment by people who really know what they are doing."

Matt read the rhyme aloud a second time. "According to this we have to remove them, not destroy them."

"Get them out of Scarr's reach and then call the federal authorities," said Jarro. "That's the way to go."

Targon groaned. "Pity we don't know where the CGP's are anymore."

"How many crates were there?" asked Matt.

"I counted eighteen."

"Eighteen!" everyone screamed in unison.

"Jeepers," said Jarro. "And they're on this island?"

"Ah! But they won't be as difficult to find as you think," said Varl.

Everyone stopped and looked at him.

"Got an idea?" asked Matt.

"Think about it," said Varl. "Targon saw eighteen CGP's and a load of booty in the tomb late afternoon yesterday. Yet early this morning everything was gone. That's a huge amount of stuff that was moved in just a few hours."

"And the rhyme says the CGP's are heavy," added Targon.

"And therefore they're probably not far," said Jarro with a broad smile.

"Get the maps," said Varl. "We've got some work to do."

"No need for that," said Targon. "If Mowann Kimile *is* involved I'll bet you anything I know exactly where the CGP's are."

Chapter 15

Gabriela sat hugging her knees at the base of Balamachu. Dusk was fast approaching and she was still fighting back tears, but she wasn't ready to go home.

How could Targon have turned on her? How could he have said those things about her father? How could he have lied to her about what he had seen in the tomb? And yet deep inside, she had the awful feeling that he was right and that her father *was* involved somehow.

She opened her bag and pulled out a tissue and the flashlight. Perhaps she would find some clue in the tomb that would tell her one way or another for certain. Perhaps there was something they missed this morning. She blew her nose and left her bag in the grass where she had sat. Then, drawing in a deep breath she walked over to the steps and climbed the pyramid. She had done this so many times that it didn't prove difficult even in the low light. She reached the entrance to the tomb and hovered on the top step.

The powerful flashlight beam guided her way down the tortuous steps. She turned it off when she reached the bottom, and stood in the darkness wondering if the spirit of Queen Elena might appear. But she didn't come.

Gabriela turned the flashlight back on and walked

over to the gate. She gripped the metal railings and shook the gate fiercely, but it wouldn't open. Surely there had to be some clue down here! How about on the ground? She shone her flashlight around the area, but nothing caught her attention.

She was about to go back up the steps when she heard voices and saw lights flickering above. Someone was coming down the steps! Her heart skipped a beat. Was it Targon? Or was it the pirates? What should she do?

She remembered Targon's story of how he had hidden in the far corner of the entrance to the tomb, and quickly found the recess in the wall that he had described. She turned off her light and waited, listening to her heart pounding.

The voices grew louder but Gabriela didn't recognize any of them. She decided that she could hear at least four different people.

"So Skimmy, this is becoming a regular trip for you."

"Twice in two days ain't bad, O'Malley," said Skimmy in his high-pitched voice. "But I ain't had this much booty to carry in weeks. Are you okay, Billy? I can hear your heavy breathing."

"Nah, I'm fine. The sun wasn't out this time," replied Billy in a distinct husky voice that Gabriela knew she wouldn't forget.

"So Hawkeye, it was a profitable raid last night with the senator onboard." Gabriela recognized O'Malley's low silky voice easily—he used proper grammar and seemed more educated than the others.

"Yeah, our contact on Moji did a good job. Heck, he always does a good job getting us information," Hawkeye laughed. "We've taken riches from celebrities and prominent politicians alike. Don't matter where it comes from, does it?"

"I think it does. I feel like Robin Hood. We only take from the very rich."

"Skimmy, you're just soft."

Gabriela held her breath when she realized that the group had reached the bottom of the steps. She prayed the beams from their flashlights wouldn't shine in her direction.

"Where's the stupid spirit, Skimmy?"

"Be patient, Billy. She always comes."

There was silence.

"Well, she don't seem to be coming," said Hawkeye.

"Patience. Have patience," said Skimmy.

There was another minute of silence.

"Spirit of Queen Elena. Are you there? We need to enter the tomb," said Skimmy.

"What's happening, Skimmy? Is the spirit here or ain't she?" Gabriela decided that was the voice of the one they called Hawkeye. His voice was thick and throaty.

"Don't know. This ain't happened to us before," said Skimmy.

"Why don't you shine the flashlights on the tomb?" suggested O'Malley.

"You alright down there, Hawkeye?" a concerned

voice shouted down from outside.

"Yeah, Elrod, we're fine," replied Hawkeye. "Stay put. Okay, everyone, do as O'Malley suggested and shine the lights on the tomb."

Suddenly there were gasps and foul language.

"It's gone! The booty's gone!" shouted Billy. "It's all gone!"

There was a commotion and Skimmy yelled, "Take it easy, boss! Take it easy! You're strangling me!"

"What you done with it all, Skimmy? I'm gonna kill you and Billy, both! You were here last!"

"Hawkeye, let him go," said O'Malley in a very controlled tone. "Stop and think about this for a minute. Don't you think that Billy and Skimmy would be long gone by now if they'd taken all the loot? Besides, you don't think these two are capable of organizing something so clever, do you?"

"Thanks a lot, O'Malley," said Skimmy. "Though I somehow think that was an insult. How do we know that *you* didn't take it all, O'Malley—you being so clever an' all!"

"Hey! Calm down, Skimmy! Someone get him off me! I don't want to punch a kid!" shouted O'Malley.

Gabriela watched the beam from one of the flashlights move violently in every direction. What was happening? Perhaps if she leaned forward a little she would be able to see . . . As she shifted her position her hand knocked against the tomb wall. Loose rock cascaded to the ground. She caught her breath.

"Hey, Hawkeye! Did you hear that?" said Billy.

"What?"

"Over there!"

Then there was silence. Gabriela watched the shadows in the half-light. Everyone was standing still. Her heart pounded so fast that she wondered if it would fail. Suddenly four bright beams of light focused on her. She froze. Then one beam shone at her face, blinding her.

"Well, lookee, lookee! What have we got here?" said Hawkeye, pulling her away from the wall. "It's Mowann Kimile's girl, little missy Gabriela Kimile, ain't it?"

Gabriela tried to push him away but he tightened his grip on her arm. His breath stank and the black patch across his eye made him look quite fierce in the gloom.

"You have no idea who I am!" she said indignantly.

"You look just like your father," Hawkeye said, fingering her long hair.

"And how would you know?" she spat.

"'Cause Cap'n Scarr has a picture of you in his cabin."

Gabriela shuddered. "And why would that be?"

"'Cause the cap'n likes to know the families of those he's dealin' with."

"Dealing with?" said Gabriela.

"Your old man's a friend of the cap'n."

"So Mowann Kimile is the contact on Moji," said O'Malley.

"And he's mighty good at getting us the information

we need," said Hawkeye.

Gabriela felt like someone had just punched her in the stomach. So it was true! Her father *had* betrayed her! How *could* he work with pirates?

"Could it not have been Kimile who moved the booty?" suggested O'Malley in his upper-class accent.

"That dirty double-crosser!" shouted Hawkeye. "I'll bet anything it's him!"

"I say we take her back to the *Dreamseeker* as a hostage," said Billy. "Ain't no one going to get away with stealing from Billy Rogers!"

"But don't hurt her," said Skimmy. "It ain't her fault that she's got a double-crossing dad."

"Now why would I hurt a lovely young lady like this 'un?" said Hawkeye. "Anyone would think I was some kind of monster." He shoved her toward the steps.

"Go easy, Hawkeye," said Skimmy. "Billy's already caused one accident down here."

"Well, the man didn't die, did he?" said Hawkeye. "Or else where's the body? But Missy Kimile here—she just might not be as lucky. Depends on what her old man tells us about the booty."

Gabriela choked back a scream. But as she climbed the steps out of the tomb her anger took over from her fear. She boiled inside. Her father had put her life in danger. And all for what? Money? Money that they already had plenty of.

* * * * *

Targon stood in front of Balamachu with Matt, Varl
and Jarro gathered in a semicircle around him. The night
was black except for the light from the quarter-moon and
their flashlights.

"Balamachu was actually once a city," he told them.

"That's correct," said Jarro. "Although these days we
refer to this, the largest pyramid, as Balamachu."

"There were another four pyramids built," continued
Targon. "Three are now just a heap of moss-covered
stones, but the fourth one is still okay. Gabriela said that
her father only closed it off last year because the steps
were almost worn away."

"So where is this fourth tomb?" asked Varl.

"I was standing exactly where we are now with
Gabriela and she pointed to another tomb over there," he
said, gesturing. "I could see it quite clearly through the
trees in daylight, so it can't be far."

"How did they get trucks up here from the coast to
bring in the CGP's?" asked Matt.

"I doubt they used trucks—it would be too hard with
the dense undergrowth," said Jarro. "They had to have
brought the CGP's in by plane, and there *is* an
abandoned air force base about two miles from here."

"And then the other night they had to move them
again," said Targon. "How could they have done that?"

"Do you think the fourth tomb is close enough to walk
to carrying heavy weapons?" asked Matt.

"Sure," said Targon. "But you'd need a lot of men to move the amount of stuff that I saw."

Jarro shook his head. "Not a problem for a man like Mowann Kimile. He could easily rally a large number of men in a hurry."

"Well, let's not waste any more time," said Varl. "Let's go see for ourselves."

Targon started to lead the way when he tripped over something in the grass and fell flat on his face.

Matt rushed to his aid. "You okay?"

"What's this?" said Targon, shining his flashlight down on the ground. He gasped. "It's Gabriela's bag!"

"Are you sure?" asked Varl.

Targon picked up and unzipped the fabric shoulder bag. "It's hers, alright. The flashlight is gone, but here are the bottles of water she packed for us this morning. And look! Her wallet is still inside!"

"She must have come here after she ran from Lara's cottage this morning," said Varl.

"I guess she came to look in the tomb again," said Targon. "I hope she's okay. I feel really badly for saying what I did about her father."

"You had no choice," said Varl. "Sometimes the truth hurts."

"Do you think she went inside the tomb?" asked Matt.

"Well, she took the flashlight out of her bag, which would suggest just that," said Varl. "Boys, you'd better check it out before we go anywhere. Just in case she's fallen down the steps." He touched his head. "You don't mind if I stay here, do you?"

Targon didn't answer. He was already climbing the pyramid with Matt on his heels. What if something had happened to Gabriela? He'd never forgive himself.

Chapter 16

M owann Kimile paced in front of his desk. He looked at his watch, again. This was so unlike Gabriela to disobey him. Where was she? He pulled off his glasses and rubbed his tired eyes. Until that darn boy arrived everything had been just fine. In the last twenty-four hours he'd done nothing but damage control—and all because of the boy!

His walkie-talkie buzzed. He ran around to his desk drawer and took out the tiny device. "Finally, Scarr!" he growled. "I've been trying to reach you since late last night! We've got serious problems. We've got a meddling boy who's seen too much."

He listened intently to Scarr, his rage growing by the minute. "You've done what? You've got to be joking! Send the jolly boat for me. I'll be at Devil's Cove in an hour."

* * * * *

Matt collapsed in the grass below the pyramid, gasping. That pyramid was one spooky place, he thought, but at least he and Targon had checked inside for Gabriela.

"She's not there," Targon told Varl and Jarro.

"Well, at least she's not lying at the bottom of the steps," said Varl.

"But where is she?" asked Targon. "I have a really bad feeling because she left her bag here."

Matt shuddered, remembering how he'd felt when Bronya was dragged off to Central Jail for helping him in Level 4 of his *Keeper of the Kingdom* game. "Don't worry, Targon. We'll find her."

"But not now," said Varl. "We must find these CGP's and stop Scarr, or we'll have much more to worry about than Gabriela."

"Gabriela knows the area well," added Jarro. "If she's anything like her father, she's a survivor and she'll be okay. We'll look for her later."

Targon sighed. "Okay. Let's go to the other pyramid."

Matt walked alongside his friend, trying to cheer him up. Things were starting to come together but he still had a long way to go to win Level 5.

They reached the fourth pyramid in just over five minutes. It was smaller than Balamachu, but of the same construction and design.

Matt shone his flashlight on the steps. "They're in pretty bad shape," he said.

"Sorry, boys, you're on your own," Varl declared. "I've not fully recovered from the first fall, so there's no way I'm going up there."

"I'll go with them," said Jarro.

Matt took off his backpack. "Will you watch my

laptop?" he asked Varl.

"You don't think I'd let it out of my sight, do you?"

Matt laughed. "Not if you know what's good for you."

He watched as his old friend took a seat on the bottom step of the pyramid and then he started to climb. Targon and Jarro were already halfway up, but he quickly caught up with them.

It took some nerve going down into the tomb. Matt kept his left hand pressed firmly against the outer wall to steady himself. Finally they reached the bottom.

He wiped the sweat from his forehead. "Zang it! Am I ever glad that—"

Boom! There was a loud bang followed by a flash of bright light. He jumped back. For a few seconds he was blinded. But when his eyes had adjusted, he could see a woman standing in front of him, shrouded in pink light. She wore a white robe and had long dark hair, just as Targon had described.

Matt instantly thought Targon was wrong, and that the spirit was a hologram. After all, he'd already met two holograms in his computer game, so why not a third?

He reached out to touch her arm and gulped when his hand met something firm and flesh-like. But her skin was icy cold—not warm like his own.

"I am the Gate Keeper of Balamachu, the spirit of Queen Elena. Who are you who dares to enter the tomb of King Bakana Kimile, first leader of the Kayapuche tribe?"

"It's Targon, Matt and Jarro," said Targon.

"Please state your business with the king," said the spirit.

"We wish to make an offering to King Bakana," said Targon.

"What is the password for entrance into the burial chamber?"

"Dreamseeker," said Targon.

Matt watched and listened carefully to everything that happened, taking in every detail.

Queen Elena waved her arms in a figure eight above her head, and a heavy black gate swung open. "You may enter, but do not remove anything from the tomb, or there will be consequences."

As the orange lamps illuminated the room, Matt could hardly believe what he saw. The tomb was full of riches—piles of money and sparkling diamonds that looked as though they had been dumped in a hurry. But at the far end, stacked carefully against the wall, were several large metal crates, each bearing the letters CGP and the word DANGER in red on the side. Matt counted them—there were eighteen. He knew instantly what he was looking at. Suddenly the threat posed by Persivius Scarr seemed very real.

Jarro stood next to Targon as if in a trance. "Jeez," he muttered. "I would never have believed it if I weren't seeing it with my own eyes."

Matt left them examining the crates. He decided he wanted to get a better look at Queen Elena. Something about her didn't seem quite right. He found her still standing outside the gate in the same position, but now she wasn't moving so much as a finger. Matt wasn't sure if he believed in spirits, but something seemed phony about Elena. The feel of her skin had given him chills, and besides, how could she be a spirit if she were a solid form?

He walked back through the gate and touched her again. She tipped her head and smiled at him in a robotic way. Matt walked behind her. She didn't ask him what he was doing or turn her head to watch him. It all seemed very odd.

Matt studied her white robe. Was that a big rectangular box showing through the fabric covering her back? He looked more closely. It was a power pack! Elena was no spirit! And she was no hologram! Neither was she made of metal like the Cybergons in Zaul. Her flesh looked human—even though it didn't feel human—and it looked as though she even had muscles and joints. Matt guessed she had been constructed from synthetic materials, with a computer for a brain.

He'd heard about technology such as this, but he'd never seen it—computer-driven electrodes linked to fabricated muscles, so that the robot's arms, legs and even fingers could move. Elena's movements mimicked the subtle movements of a human. There was no doubt that she had been cleverly put together and programmed. What an unbelievable feat of technology! If this technology was available in his own time, 2010, why shouldn't even greater advances have been made by

2540? Matt walked around her excitedly. But where was the computer that programmed her, and where had Elena come from so suddenly?

He remembered the loud bang and flash that had announced Elena's arrival. It was a good cover. He shone his flashlight around the enclosure, directing the beam up at every crevice. Wait—was that a crack in the rock? Matt ran his hand down a thin seam in the stonework and then found a second seam several feet from the first. There was a trap door in the tomb! It must be where Elena was kept in between her appearances. He pushed on the wall but nothing happened. *Computer controlled,* he thought.

"Jarro! Targon! Come here!" yelled Matt.

"What is it?" asked Targon.

"Doesn't something strike you as odd?" asked Matt.

"How do you mean?" said Targon.

"So many things about Elena just don't add up. For example, Elena asked exactly the same things today as you told me she'd asked you before, and she gave you the same answers."

"So?" said Targon.

"I see what Matt's getting at," said Jarro. "This is *not* the tomb of King Bakana Kimile, and yet that's what Queen Elena said it was."

"Exactly," said Matt. "She's been moved here but her program hasn't been changed."

"So she's not a spirit then," said Targon. "Is she a hologram?"

"No, she's not that, either. She's basically a robot."

Matt could instantly feel Targon's panic.

"L . . . like the C . . .Cybergons?" Targon stammered.

"The Cybergons?" said Jarro.

"No, nothing like the Cybergons," Matt reassured him, ignoring Jarro's question. There was no way he wanted to recount the tale of horror from Level 1 of his computer game. "I'm guessing that Elena is controlled by a computer, which is programmed by the person who moved the CGP's here last night."

"Mowann Kimile," said Targon.

"Elena is his watchdog so he had to move her here along with the booty and the CGP's," continued Matt. "The rhyme said that we wouldn't be able to remove the weapons from the tomb without deactivating the Keeper, and Elena warned us that we weren't to take anything from the tomb."

"What will happen if we do?" asked Targon.

Matt shook his head. "I haven't figured that out yet."

Jarro walked over to Elena. He touched her and laughed. "So why not pull off her power pack right now?" he said, his hand on her back. "I can see it right here."

"Please remove your hand," said Elena. "If you try to remove my power, I will self-destruct. The tomb will implode and you will all die."

"Not to mention what might happen to the CGP's—kaboom!" said Matt.

Jarro moved back instantly. "I guess there's our answer. Death by burial would not be nice!"

"And I'll bet that if we took anything from the tomb

she'd also self-destruct, setting off a massive explosion," said Matt.

"But how would she know?" asked Targon.

"Scarr has probably installed weight sensors under the entrance. If the person leaving the tomb is heavier than when they went into the tomb, it would register on her computer."

"Is that how she knows when to appear?" asked Targon.

"Maybe Scarr installed weight sensors at the bottom of the steps as well," said Jarro.

"Or it could be that Elena is sound-activated or motion-activated when someone enters the pyramid," said Matt. "And another thing—don't you think it would be a little difficult to get the CGP's up and down these worn-down twisting steps? I mean, you've just seen them—they're in huge crates!"

"I've been thinking about that," said Jarro. "Have you come up with an answer?"

Matt touched the wall. "There's a secret panel right here. It won't open, but I'm guessing it might lead to a tunnel between the tombs."

"That's how they could move the CGP's easily and quickly," said Targon.

"And we all thought Elena appeared by magic. But the crash and the flash of light would prevent us from seeing her coming in and out of this secret place."

"I'm impressed, Matt," said Jarro. "You've pieced this all together and it does seem plausible."

"So where's the computer that programmed her?" said Matt. "That's the question."

"In Mowann Kimile's study, I'll bet you anything," said Targon. "I saw two huge screens and two keyboards on his desk. He even turned one of the screens off when Gabriela walked behind his desk the other night."

"Well, let's start there," said Matt.

"And do what, exactly?" asked Jarro.

"There has to be a small wireless device inside Elena that receives signals from the main computer. If Targon can get me close enough to the Kimile house, I'll hack into the wireless system using my laptop and try to reprogram the software."

"You know how to do all that?" asked Jarro.

"It depends upon how advanced his computer network is," said Matt. "In fact, it would be even better if we could get inside his house so that I can use his computer."

"I think the housekeeper liked me," said Targon. "I'm sure I can persuade her to let me in."

"What should I do in the meantime?" asked Jarro.

"Do you know which authorities you can trust—who aren't working for Scarr?"

"I can think of at least five people," said Jarro.

"Good. Can you get an armed guard on this tomb? I'll be able to meet up with Conan O'Malley tomorrow. He'll know where to take these CGP's for safe detonation. If I can deactivate Elena, then the authorities can move the CGP's tomorrow."

"Done," said Jarro. "I can be back here within the hour."

"Right, who's going to tell Varl what we've discovered?" said Matt. "He'll be fascinated."

"I will," said Targon. "He'll say, 'That's technology for you, my boy!'"

They all laughed.

As Matt walked back down the pyramid steps, waving to Varl below, he had a sinking feeling. Deactivating Elena would not be an easy task. What if Mowann Kimile's computer system was as sophisticated as the one onboard the *Dreamseeker*? What would he do then?

Chapter 17

"Let go of me!" Gabriela twisted painfully to try and shake free of Scarr's grip. What a revolting man!

"You're a pretty child," said Scarr, his foul breath spraying her face. "In fact, you're prettier than in this 'ere photo." He grabbed it off the desk and showed it to her. "It'd be a mighty shame if somethin' were to 'appen to you."

Gabriela leaned back away from his reeking breath.

"What's the matter? You think you're too good for the likes of me?"

"You smell like you haven't washed in weeks!" spat Gabriela. "No woman in her right mind would want to go near you."

Scarr threw her to the floor of his cabin. "You brat! There's me tryin' me best to be nice to you."

"Get lost, you creep!" shouted Gabriela.

"Now that weren't nice, neither," Scarr hissed. "Your father will be 'ere any time, an' then we'll 'ear what 'e's got to say for 'imself."

The cabin door opened.

"Speak of the devil," said Scarr. "'ere 'e is."

"Gabriela, my dear! Are you okay? I hope these men

didn't hurt you." Her father bent to help her off the floor.

Gabriela pushed him away and stood up of her own accord. "Cut the act, Father! How could you?" she screamed, backing up. "How could you deal with these dirty scumbags?"

"Gabriela, dear," he said, walking towards her again.

She backed against the windows, almost falling into the window seat. "Don't you dare lie to me, Father. I know all about the booty at Balamachu. Targon told me everything. I can't believe that you put my life at risk for a load of money. We already have plenty!"

"It's not like that, really," her father said. "It's not about money for us. I'm doing something I believe is essential to ensure the future of these islands—something that will benefit the poor people of Moji. There are lots of things you don't know."

"But they be things I do wanna know about," growled Scarr.

"We can talk about this later," said her father.

"Where are me CGP's?" continued Scarr. "Did you double-cross me, or what?"

"What do you think I am?" said her father. "Stupid? I gave you my word. But we've got problems that have to be dealt with."

"So you said. The meddlin' boy, Targon, for one."

"If you'd answered my calls last night, you would have known in time and none of this would have happened today."

"I 'ad a big job to do last night, as well you know. It

took all of me attention."

Her father glared at Scarr. "And you couldn't answer my calls this morning, either?"

"This ship don't run 'erself. We've tourists to prepare for."

"Do we have to go into this with my daughter in the room?"

"Why wouldn't you, Father? Are you afraid that I'll hear the truth and not like what I hear?" asked Gabriela.

"'awkeye, lock 'er in the brig," said Scarr.

"Please," said her father, stepping between Hawkeye and Gabriela. "There's no need for that."

"But there is," said Scarr. "I want the problem gone and until it is, your daughter stays with me."

"She's just a child and she's not involved."

"She is now," said Scarr. "So you'd better get back to the mainland and get rid of the boy, for starters. After all, it was Miss Kimile who brought the boy to you in the first place."

"And if she hadn't done so, we'd never have known the problems we had until it was too late," pleaded her father. "At least I've been able to do damage control. Have some compassion, Scarr."

"I'll 'ave some compassion when you've dealt with the problem completely. 'Til then she's me security." Scarr drew his pistol. "Now move out of the way, Kimile."

Her father didn't budge. "You can't kill me," he said. "Without my computer programming you can't get your CGP's from the tomb. They're stuck there."

Scarr moved the barrel of the pistol until it was pointing at Gabriela. "That may be so, but I could start by shootin' your daughter's leg an' then 'er arm and then 'er stomach. A slow, painful, agonizin' end . . . What will 'er dear mother say when she returns from 'er trip and finds bullet 'oles all over 'er little Gabriela's body?"

"Enough! I'll do what you want. Just don't hurt my daughter."

"You keep your part of the deal and she'll be fine," said Scarr. "Double-cross me and she's fish food!"

Gabriela shuddered. She was so disgusted she couldn't even look at her father as Hawkeye led her from Scarr's cabin. And now it seemed Targon would have to die if she were to live.

* * * * *

Matt stood outside Mowann Kimile's elegant white house. "It's a bit different from every other house on the street."

"That's what you get for being the mayor of Moji," said Targon.

"And leader of the Kayapuche tribe," added Matt. "There's obviously lots of family money—if you think about all the land he owns."

"There are lights on," said Targon. "So someone's up. I wonder if Gabriela got home safely."

"Where's the study?" asked Matt.

"It's on the ground floor at that end of the house."

Targon pointed to the right-hand side of the building.

"If you could get into the house and then open one of the study windows for me, I could do what I have to do without anyone knowing I'm even there."

"Unless Mowann Kimile is working late."

"Well, then we've got a problem and I'll just have to try and hack into the system from out here," said Matt.

Targon looked down at Gabriela's bag in his hand. "This is a great excuse to knock on the door, even if it is nearly midnight."

"Well, let's try it," said Matt. "You ready?"

Targon nodded. "Might as well try. Though I can't really say I want to see Mr. Kimile, knowing what I do."

Matt ducked below the front bushes and watched Targon climb the steps to the front door. He could hear the heavy timbers resound with Targon's footsteps—very different from the crunching of the rotting wood on Lara's front porch.

Targon rang the bell and a loud melodic chime sounded. A plump dark-skinned woman in a robe came to the door. She looked as though she'd been crying.

"Amelia," said Targon. "Are you okay? Did Gabriela get home safely tonight?"

Amelia shook her head and wiped her eyes on the sleeve of her robe. "No, *ella no volvió,* Mr. Targon. She not return. Her momma's gonna be so angry with me when she gets home. I was supposed to look after her."

Targon held up the bag. "I found her bag tonight at Balamachu. I'm worried about her."

Amelia gasped and covered her mouth with her hands. "Oh my goodness! *Dios Mio!* I sure hopes nothing bad has happened to Miss Gabriela. Mr. Kimile has gone out, but he's bin real worried all evening. He'll want to know what you seen. *Venido adentro.* Come in, Mr. Targon. Come in and wait for him!"

Perfect, thought Matt. He waited until the door closed and then crept through the darkness around the side of the porch to the far end of the house. Suddenly a light shone through two windows and one of the windows opened.

"Fresh air!" Matt heard Targon say. "That's better. It was so stuffy in here."

"I hope Mr. Kimile will not mind me letting you in his study," Amelia said.

"I won't touch anything, I promise," said Targon. "I'd like to look at the books, if that's okay."

"I guess it be alright. Now I going back in the kitchen—just in case Miss Gabriela comes home. She always comes in that way. An' I'll leave some sandwiches out for you. *Buenos noches*, Mr. Targon."

"*Buenos noches*, Amelia."

Targon appeared at the window. "All clear," he said. "But we'll have to keep watch—she didn't completely close the study door."

Matt reached for Targon's hand. "Careful, my computer's in my backpack." He hauled himself through the window.

The study was both bigger and more luxurious than

Matt had imagined. He approached the desk and looked at the computer screens. They were turned off. The keyboard was pretty much what he was used to, but where was the hard drive?

"See anything like a computer?" he asked Targon. "I can't hack into the system if it's not turned on. Where would Kimile keep it?"

They opened up the cupboards under the desk, and even behind the books.

"This is crazy," said Matt, checking the desk drawers. "Where is it? Aha! Found it!"

He pulled a silver box out of the drawer. It was a quarter of the size of his laptop with a switch on one side, several infrared ports on the other and a small slot, which Matt assumed was equivalent to his PMCIA card slot.

"Zang it! What a tiny thing," said Targon. "Are you sure that's it?"

"Sure I'm sure," said Matt. "Watch the screens. Here we go." He turned on the switch and then pressed the buttons under the screens. They both illuminated immediately. "Good, we're in business." He sat down in Kimile's leather chair in front of his sophisticated silver keyboard. "First thing to do is log on."

"You need a password, right?" asked Targon.

"Now you're learning. This might take some time. What do you think Kimile would use?"

Targon laughed. "That's an easy one. Try 'Gabriela.'"

Matt chuckled. He typed in Gabriela and her photo filled the screen for a few seconds. Then a menu appeared. "Glad I've got you with me! He's not a very shrewd businessman, is he? Shall I change his password for him?"

Targon leaned over Matt as he was working. "Can you really do that?"

"Just did," said Matt. "And he'll never figure it out."

"It's Matt1," said Targon.

Matt shot him a dumbfounded look. "How did you know that?"

"In Level 4, Jake told me to tell you that you had to change your password because it was dumb and anyone could get it. I guess you'd better learn your own lesson!"

"I'll change it later," said Matt, embarrassed by his own stupidity. "Okay, let's deactivate this Keeper so that I can concentrate on the one on the *Dreamseeker* that'll give me more problems."

Targon smiled at him. "I'm glad that I've not got to go back to the *Dreamseeker* tomorrow," he said. "What are you planning on doing to deactivate Elena?"

"In five minutes I can't do anything that's a permanent fix. The computer language might be difficult to read. So I'm just going to turn off the program. And because I've now changed the password, Kimile won't be able to get back in and turn the program back on again."

"Will it take long?"

"It will if you keep talking to me," said Matt, hammering away at the keys. "Check the door, will you? I think I hear something."

Targon came running back. "Mowann Kimile's home."

"Zang it!" said Matt. "I'm not done. You'll just have to stall him."

"Stall him?"

"Just do anything to keep him out of here!"

Chapter 18

Targon closed the study door and walked into the entrance hall just in time to hear Amelia say to Mowann Kimile, "Mr. Targon is waiting for you in the study, sir."

"Thank you, Amelia. I'll see you in the morning."

Targon drew in a deep breath and studied the man's expression, trying to decide how best to approach him. He wasn't as stern-looking as he had been the day before, but neither was he as friendly-looking as he had been at breakfast. In fact, Targon thought the man looked positively ill—but that was probably because he was so worried about his daughter.

"I found Gabriela's bag, Mr. Kimile," said Targon, handing him the bag before the man had a chance to open his mouth. "I found it this evening at Balamachu and I was worried about her. I even checked down inside the tomb in case she'd fallen down the steps—but there was no sign of her."

Mowann Kimile exhaled deeply and drew himself upright. "It was kind of you to come by tonight," he said. "Shall we go into the study?"

"Actually, can we go into the kitchen?" said Targon, already walking in that direction. "Amelia said she'd made me some sandwiches."

"Oh . . . um . . . alright," Kimile said, although his body language said otherwise. "Though we could take it into the study."

"No, I like the kitchen," said Targon forcefully. That sounded rude, he thought and so he added, "Gabriela might come back at any time and she usually comes in that way, doesn't she?"

Mowann Kimile frowned. He seemed confused by Targon's answer, but followed him into the kitchen.

"So you weren't with my daughter all day," he said.

Targon sat down at the kitchen table and took a chicken sandwich from the plate in the middle. "No, she left me at lunchtime."

"Oh, that's a pity," said Kimile.

Targon thought it a strange comment when the man obviously didn't like him. "Yes, I suppose she'd be here right now if we'd stayed together," he said.

"I couldn't find any information about your friend, Varl. I'm sorry."

"That's okay," said Targon, wiping his mouth on a napkin. "I found him."

Mowann Kimile nearly shot out of his chair. "You did? Where?"

"In the village of Cala de la Tortuga."

"So your whole experience in the tomb was just a figment of your imagination?" said Kimile, his face brightening. "And you can now forget the whole thing and carry on with your vacation."

"Not at all," said Targon. "Varl was seriously injured.

If it hadn't been for a healer in the village, he'd be dead."

"Really," said Mowann Kimile, sounding stern again. "And where is he now?"

"Still in Cala de la Tortuga."

"Are you certain of your facts?"

"You bet. Tomorrow I'm going to the police. I'll get these men put away for what they did. I know their names, I know about some weapons they have called CGP's, and I even know what boat they're on."

Mowann Kimile leaped to his feet. "You do, do you?"

"Sure," said Targon, shifting uncomfortably with Kimile's change in tone and stance. He'd been stupid revealing how much he knew, but he'd enjoyed watching Mowann Kimile squirm—and at least he'd made him forget about going into the study. "Well, it's very late. I'm going. I hope you find Gabriela in the morning." He stood up and started for the kitchen door.

Suddenly Kimile blocked his route, grabbed a knife from the block on the countertop and lunged at him. "You're not going anywhere. You know too much. Now walk into my study, and don't make a sound."

Fear paralyzed Targon. He felt faint. He'd gone too far.

Mowann Kimile held the knife to his throat and frog-marched him across the hall and through the study doors. Targon held his breath as they entered the room. There was no sign of Matt. Where was he?

Targon saw that the window was closed. Had Matt successfully deactivated Elena and gone back to the tomb?

Kimile pushed Targon into a chair at the side of his desk. Still holding the knife at Targon's throat, he fumbled in one of his desk drawers. "Where's the tape?" he muttered.

"I don't understand what I've done," said Targon.

"You really are a dim kid," said Mowann Kimile. "If you'd just left things alone, agreed to go off on vacation, and forgotten what you'd seen—like any normal person would have done—I could have let you go. But, no, you had to persist, didn't you? Scarr won't have his pirating operation exposed, and he's holding my daughter hostage. I'm sorry, but it's your life or hers!"

Targon swallowed. "So what are you going to do—kill me?"

"Whatever else you think I am, I'm not a murderer. I'll give you to Scarr in exchange for my daughter and he can do as he pleases."

"You're still a murderer—you just let other people do the murdering for you," said Targon. "Like helping Scarr hide his CGP's. Those things will kill millions."

"I'm just creating wealth for the poor people of this island the only way I know how. Scarr gives me 30 percent of everything he collects. In a few years I'll have enough to build a new port for the cruise ships and invest heavily in the island businesses that serve the tourist trade."

"Yeah, right. And you don't care about the people you're hurting in the process," said Targon. "We *can* do a deal, Mr. Kimile."

"It's way too late for that," he replied, pulling out the tape. He slapped a long piece across Targon's mouth.

Targon's mind was in turmoil. Dare he tackle a man who was twice his size and who was holding a serrated kitchen knife at his throat? Within ten seconds his hands would be taped to the chair. He watched Mowann Kimile pick up the roll of tape. It was now or never!

Suddenly there was a loud thump. Targon drew back, startled. Mowann Kimile's eyes glazed over, his mouth gaped and the knife fell from his hand. He staggered for a few seconds and then fell flat on his face across the desk. He was out cold.

Targon looked up to see Matt wielding one of the bronze statues from the bookcase. "Now who's dim, *Mr. Kimile?*" he said, ripping the tape off Targon's mouth. "Don't worry, I didn't kill him. Just side-swiped him."

Targon was shaking. "I thought you'd gone," he said.

"What, and leave you here? I was under the desk the whole time."

"Thanks," said Targon. "You saved my life."

"No time for that," said Matt. "He'll come around before we know it. Let's tie up his hands and feet and gag him. We'll find something stronger than that tape. There has to be some rope out back."

"And then what? Cook will be here in a couple of hours to start breakfast," said Targon.

"We'll find a faraway closet to put him in—somewhere in the house where neither Amelia nor the cook will go. Jarro can come over here at daybreak with the police and arrest Mowann Kimile."

"Let's do it," said Targon.

* * * * *

"A new day," said Matt, as he walked along the seafront path with Targon. He wondered what *this* day would bring. He tried to enjoy the dawn sky and the melodic bird songs, but he found himself racing, anxious to get back to the tomb.

"So you never told me," said Targon. "Did you manage to deactivate Elena?"

"I did get into Kimile's computer and I managed to turn off the program. Elena should be deactivated. I'm just hoping that by turning off the program the gate will be permanently open. I guess we'll know in a minute."

As they approached, Matt was relieved to see a large group of armed men standing with Jarro. Many of them were also in uniform.

"Boys, you're back," said Varl, walking to meet them. "As you can see, Jarro has gathered quite a team. He's also got the Chief of Police here and a number of trustworthy officers."

"That's great," said Matt.

"The question is, did you succeed in deactivating the Keeper?" whispered Varl.

"I hope so," said Matt. "Mowann Kimile came home

and I was under pressure to get it done."

Varl looked alarmed. "You both okay?"

Targon pulled a face. "Only just—but it's a long story that can wait."

Matt drew in a deep breath. "Okay, let's go down into the tomb and see if I succeeded."

Jarro approached. "Any luck?"

"I'm about to find out," said Matt.

"I'll come too," said Jarro.

"Before I forget, you'll find Mowann Kimile tied up and gagged in one of his bedroom closets," said Matt.

"I'll get over there with the Chief when we're done here," said Jarro.

"Let him have an uncomfortable night first," Targon said angrily. "The man deserves it." He touched the spot where the knife had been against his throat.

Jarro laughed. "Okay, I'll leave it a few hours."

Matt sighed. "If all goes well Conan O'Malley will be here tomorrow. It'll be a federal case then."

"There's a lot of people on this island who'll be pleased to see Mowann Kimile put away," said Jarro.

This time Matt easily navigated the pyramid steps. Am I more confident, he thought, or just anxious to get inside? He didn't even bother looking back at Varl.

Jarro reached the bottom first and shone his flashlight around. "No Elena," he said.

"I guess that's a good sign," said Targon.

Jarro shone his beam at the black gate. "It's still closed," he said sadly.

"But is it locked?" asked Matt. He gave the gate a tug. It opened with ease and the orange lights illuminated the room as if by magic.

Jarro laughed. "You're a genius, boy!"

"No, just good with computers," said Matt.

Jarro stroked his stubbled chin. "But how do we know if you disabled Elena and if we're going to be able to remove the CGP's safely?"

"I'm pretty sure that if the gate isn't locked, it means I successfully turned off the program," said Matt.

"I hope you're right," said Jarro. "It would be awful if we started to remove the CGP's and the whole pyramid came down on us. Not to mention the damage to the whole of Moji and beyond if those weapons explode."

Matt knew there was a lot at stake—in fact more than Jarro realized. If he hadn't successfully deactivated Elena he wouldn't win Level 5 of his game.

He walked over to the two seams he had found in the wall and pressed around the edges of both. "Zang it! Open, will you!" In frustration he began pressing every protruding stone in the center as well.

Suddenly there was a grating noise and a huge portion of the pyramid wall slid to one side. Standing to attention, like a stiff doll wearing a blank expression, was Elena.

"There's your answer," said Matt proudly. He was also very relieved.

Jarro slapped him on the back and Targon gave him a high five.

"I can see a tunnel behind," said Targon. "You were right."

Jarro moved toward the steps. "I'll get some of my men down here to see where it goes."

"I'll bet it connects the pyramids and leads out onto the road to the airbase," said Matt.

"Well, that would make transporting the CGP's a lot easier," said Jarro. "I'm sure the Chief of Police will be very interested to see all of this."

"Just as long as he understands that this is a federal case and the CGP's stay in the tomb until Conan O'Malley gets here," said Matt.

"I'll make sure of it," said Jarro, climbing the steps.

"So why do we have to wait for O'Malley for everything?" asked Targon.

"We don't want these weapons falling into the wrong hands—there are lots of terrorists besides Scarr who'd like them. The rhyme said that I could trust O'Malley and the islanders, and I do. Plus, I need O'Malley's help to get rid of the other Keeper tomorrow."

"So you really are going back onboard the *Dreamseeker* with the two o'clock tour?"

"You got it," said Matt.

"And you're coming back to Moji with the tour the day after?"

"Not exactly," said Matt. "You'll see."

"You'll find Gabriela, won't you?"

"Of course."

"I just hope that she'll be able to deal with her father

being a bad guy. I'm sure that Scarr's told her that by now."

"That's the only sad thing about putting Mowann Kimile behind bars—Gabriela will lose her father."

"Amelia hinted that Gabriela's got a good mother," said Targon. "By the way, what am I supposed to do while you're out dealing with Keeper number two?"

"Lots," said Matt. "I'm going to need you, Varl and Jarro to organize a fleet of fishing boats. They'll need to be at Bahia Del Tigre tomorrow afternoon, ready to go by two-thirty."

"Why Bahia Del Tigre?" asked Targon.

"Because it's only a five-minute boat ride from where the *Dreamseeker* has dropped anchor."

"Are you going to tell me what to expect?"

Matt shook his head. "You'll know when the boats are needed."

Targon yawned.

"That's it for tonight, or should I say today," said Matt, yawning too. "Let's take up Lara's offer and sleep on her floor for a few hours. I've gotta get some sleep before I catch the boat at two."

"I wonder how Mowann Kimile is sleeping in the closet," said Targon.

Matt laughed. "I shouldn't think he's sleeping at all!"

Chapter 19

Matt clutched his ticket and waited anxiously in line for the boat to the *Dreamseeker*. Lara had managed to get him a change of clothing so that he looked more like a tourist. The white Bermuda shorts, flowery shirt and straw hat made him feel uncomfortable, but at least he blended in well with everyone else waiting to board. She'd even got him a different colored backpack.

The motorboat arrived. Matt said a quick goodbye to Varl, Targon and Jarro.

Jarro shook his hand. "Good luck. We'll be waiting in a police cruiser."

"Take care, my boy," said Varl, giving him a hug. He whispered in Matt's ear, "Finish Level 5 and get us home!"

Matt smiled. "I'll do my best."

Targon came up and patted him on the back. "You won't forget about rescuing Gabriela, will you?" he said.

"Don't worry, I'll get her," said Matt as he walked up the gangplank. "Be ready at two-thirty tomorrow afternoon."

"You can count on us," said Varl.

Matt waved to them as the boat sped away from the dock at Bahia Del Tigre. He suddenly felt very alone. He was placing a lot of trust in Conan O'Malley and he hoped he wouldn't regret it.

It was a glorious day. The sky was clear blue and cloudless, and the water calm. As the motorboat turned out of the bay and headed into open water, the *Dreamseeker* came into view. She certainly was a beautiful sailing ship with her three tall masts that rose elegantly into the blue. She looked so perfect she could have been in an oil painting. If not for the roar of the motorboat engines and the chattering tourists next to him, Matt could almost believe he was in the 17th century.

But as they drew close and he could see the jolly boat hanging over her stern, his mood changed. He had a sick feeling in the pit of his stomach. How would O'Malley get him away from the tour group, especially when time was so short?

The motorboat pulled up alongside the *Dreamseeker*'s boarding ramp and cut its engines. He picked up his backpack, kept his head down and followed everyone off the little boat.

Scarr was waiting with Skimmy McFinn to greet the tourists on Orlop deck. Matt pulled down the brim of his straw hat as he shook Scarr's hand. He joined in with the group, roaring with laughter at the right moments and shouting, "Aye, me mateys," when called for. The whole time though, he kept looking over his shoulder for a glimpse of O'Malley. But O'Malley was nowhere to be seen.

Skimmy McFinn led the group up to Main deck. As always, Scarr stayed behind to see the last person in the group climb the steps. Matt realized that he was somewhere in the middle of the group of tourists. When they reached Gun deck he was surprised to see O'Malley standing by the hatch.

"Yer laces be undone, boy," he said in an exaggerated pirate accent. "Best ye stop an' tie 'em now."

Matt stepped onto Gun deck and O'Malley whisked him underneath the steps and out of view. He pushed Matt behind him as Scarr blindly followed the group up on deck.

"Thanks," said Matt after Scarr had gone.

"Good to see you again," whispered O'Malley, "though I wondered if you'd return. I thought it all might have been a bit much for you."

"Not on your life!" answered Matt. "I've got tons to tell you."

"It'll have to wait. I've got to be up on deck, and the hold is under lockdown for another eighty minutes. You'll have to find somewhere to hide."

"I've got someone to find first."

"Gabriela?" questioned O'Malley.

Matt was taken aback. "You know where she is?"

"The brig. And she'll have to stay there. If you rescue her now, Scarr will rip the ship apart looking for her."

"Tomorrow, then," said Matt. "I've got a plan and she needs to leave with us."

"We'll talk later," said O'Malley. "Got to go. Don't miss that one-minute window to get back into the hold before everyone else goes down there."

Matt watched O'Malley climb the steps up to the Main deck and then headed back down to Orlop. He decided that he'd go back and hide in the cupboard in the surgeon's cockpit. He'd just have to tolerate the rats for an hour.

* * * * *

Targon watched the motorboat disappear around the sea wall, wishing he were on it with Matt. His friend had a huge challenge ahead of him. These adventures were so much more fun when the three of them were solving problems together. He looked up at the colorful seafront, but even the bustling market and the cheerful marimba music was not enough to lift his spirits.

"Cheer up, my boy," said Varl, as if he could read his mind. "Matt is too clever for Scarr *and* he'll rescue Gabriela. Besides, we've got lots to do while he's gone."

"Bahia Del Tigre's a lovely place," said Jarro in a chirpy tone. "We can walk down by the marina and get something to eat while we're organizing fishing boats for tomorrow."

"And just how are we going to do that?" asked Targon. "Matt said he wanted at least thirty boats ready to go, and they all had to have outboard motors."

"I've already got it figured out," said Jarro. "I asked my boss at the port authority to donate a large sum of money as a prize for a fishing competition."

"And you'll hold the competition in the bay tomorrow

afternoon," said Varl.

"Exactly. My boss was so impressed when I walked into the police station with Mowann Kimile and his computer that he was quite happy to give me anything I asked for so that we could nail Scarr."

"Mowann Kimile's computer?" questioned Targon.

"Sure. There are all kinds of records on his hard drive: passenger lists from past and upcoming cruises, details of shipping routes, flight records from the deliveries of the CGP's, not to mention the program he used to operate Elena."

"All very incriminating evidence," said Varl. "The man's in it up to his eyeballs."

"Poor Gabriela," Targon cried out.

"I wouldn't worry too much," said Jarro. "Mowann Kimile will get a good lawyer who'll find a way to get the charges reduced. He'll be lucky to do ten years."

They walked up a narrow street and stopped outside a print shop. Jarro collected a pile of glossy posters advertising the fishing competition. "We'll post these around town and talk to all the fishermen and boat owners. You'll see—we'll have a ton of people with boats signed up by the end of the afternoon."

Targon smiled. "Okay," he said. "I guess we're doing something worthwhile."

"You may not be facing Persivius Scarr," said Varl, "but what we're doing here will be crucial to winning the game."

Jarro frowned. "Game? I hope it's more than that!"

"It was just a figure of speech," said Varl. He winked at Targon.

* * * * *

Gabriela was dripping with perspiration. Her clothes stuck to her and she felt dirty and disgusting. The stench of sweat and salt below deck was more than she could bear. She consoled herself with the fact that at least she liked her own company. The solitude had given her time to reflect. The pain of her father's betrayal numbed her, and she wondered if she would ever be able to forgive him for working with such a despicable man as Persivius Scarr.

And then there was Targon. In one short day he had become her friend. He had been honest with her, even if his words had been painful to hear. Her stomach churned with worry at the thought of him. She replayed Scarr's words over and over in her mind. He'd told her father to *deal* with the problem. She was not naïve—she knew what that meant. But would her father really kill for her? She couldn't allow herself to believe that he was capable of murder even to save her.

A siren blasted. Seconds later, the hatch opened and light flooded into her prison. Gabriela squinted to see who was peering down at her. She recognized the tall figure of O'Malley from the night before.

"Out with yer! Bathroom visit if yer want," he bellowed.

Suddenly his refined speech and suave behavior had been replaced by a thick pirate accent and swaggering body language. What was going on?

Gabriela climbed the ladder, stood up on Main deck and stretched her arms.

O'Malley quickly glanced over his shoulder and then leaned toward her. He whispered in her ear, "There are those onboard 'o are not with Scarr, Miss Kimile. 'ave no fear—yer'll be back on land tomorrow. Just do what yer told, when yer told, and yer'll be fine."

Gabriela tried to hide her smile, just in case anyone was watching. She nodded her understanding and walked to the tourist bathroom. Her heart fluttered and she felt on edge, not knowing how and when her rescue would happen. Had O'Malley hinted at a mutiny? As she exited the bathroom and stepped back into the fresh air, she drew in a deep breath. She probably should enjoy it—it would likely be her only glimpse of the sun until tomorrow.

O'Malley helped her back to the brig. As she climbed backward down the steps, he winked at her. The hatch closed and she sat down in semidarkness again. But her spirits were now high. She would wait patiently for her rescuers to make their move.

Chapter 20

When Matt heard the siren blast, he pushed open the cupboard and raced through the powder room and down the hatch as fast as he could. He had just reached the lockers at the stern of the hold when he heard the pirates returning from the tour. Whew! That was close.

He pulled out his pirate outfit from where he had stuffed it between two boxes. By the time that O'Malley walked through the door he had changed out of his tourist clothes and was sitting on the bench waiting for him.

"The raid tonight's been canceled," said O'Malley.

Matt laughed. "I know why. Scarr's had a few problems today. He's probably laying low until he's worked out how bad things really are."

O'Malley raised his eyebrows. "His booty has gone missing, and Gabriela Kimile's in the brig. Anything else I should know about?"

"Plenty," said Matt. "Although Scarr doesn't know half of it, of course." Immediately he recounted everything that had happened since the day before. O'Malley sat in stunned silence for a minute. Finally he said, "You seem to have achieved more in twenty-four hours than I have in months."

"But I still have one Keeper left to deal with—the

computer system here onboard," said Matt. "Then Scarr will be permanently out of business and we can hand him over to the authorities."

"And no doubt you have a plan for that too," said O'Malley.

"It's a little drastic, but if it works I guarantee that Scarr will not be pirating again. But I'll need your help to do it."

"If it's a sensible plan, I'm in," said O'Malley. "My objectives are the same as yours."

"Do you know how the airlock doors operate?"

"They're computer controlled," said O'Malley. "I realize that," said Matt. "I hate to admit it, but these computers are beyond me. I had a look at them yesterday. The program language is completely foreign, and there's no way I could hack into the system quickly and override the opening and closing of the airlock doors."

O'Malley smoothed back his hair as he always did when he was thinking. "It sounds to me as though you're intending to sink the *Dreamseeker*."

"You got it. By the time I'm done tomorrow, the *Dreamseeker* and all of Scarr's expensive equipment will be at the bottom of the ocean, completely ruined. But of course I want to do it without killing anybody onboard . . . including Scarr."

O'Malley frowned. "How do you think you can do that?"

"I watched you the other night on the raid. You operated the mini-sub."

"Indeed I did," said O'Malley. "How is that relevant?"

"You were able to open and close the airlock doors from the mini-sub."

"True. Both the computers on the mini-sub and the computers here in the hold are able to open and close both sets of airlock doors. But you can't open the outer airlock doors without first closing the inner airlock doors. That's to prevent exactly what you're describing—flooding the ship."

"Zang it!" said Matt. "I was hoping that would be our escape route too."

"Now I'm beginning to see what you're thinking," said O'Malley. "You'd do all this during lockdown when the tourists are onboard and no one else is down here. That would give you a good thirty minutes to start the flooding. By the time that everyone came back from giving the tour, the hold would be so flooded it would be too late to do anything about it. Meanwhile you'd have escaped in the mini-sub."

"*We* would have escaped in the mini-sub," corrected Matt.

"Ah!" O'Malley laughed. "It's not that you really want me along—it's just that you'd need me at the controls."

"You caught me!" Matt laughed with him for a few seconds. But suddenly a glum feeling came over him. "Anyway, all those good plans are for nothing. I'll just have to think of something else."

O'Malley got up and paced back and forth in the confined space. "There just might be a way to keep the inner airlock doors open while escaping through the outer ones," he finally said.

Matt shot off the bench. "How?"

"There are three sensors embedded along the edge of one of the inner airlock doors," said O'Malley. "When the doors close, one door pushes on the sensors in the other, and the computers register that the doors are closed."

"So how do we make the computers think the doors are closed when they aren't?"

O'Malley smiled. "We attach three thick pieces of wood to one inner airlock doors so that they're in line with the sensors on the other door."

"I get it!" said Matt. "When the blocks of wood press on the sensors they'll register that the doors have closed. But there'll actually be a gap the width of the block of wood between the two doors."

"Exactly," said O'Malley. "I can find the wood and other things we'll need later tonight."

Matt was elated. "That's the hardest part solved."

"I'm glad to hear it," said O'Malley, "because that's hard enough."

"You'll have to come up with an excuse for why you aren't on deck with everyone else helping with the tour."

O'Malley shook his head. "No good. Scarr won't accept any excuse. He won't allow anyone down here while the tour is going on. He doesn't want any noise coming up from the hold or anyone tampering with equipment. It's my job to check that everyone is out before lockdown, and then I report to him before the start of the tour."

"But that works perfectly," said Matt. "You can just be the last man to leave as usual—only tomorrow you won't actually leave."

"No good again. Scarr can override the lockdown from his cabin, should he need to."

"Then we'll just have to find a way to make everyone, including Scarr, think you're up on deck."

Suddenly O'Malley's face looked grim. "How are you going to get everyone off the ship? If the airlock doors stay open, the hold will flood pretty fast. You'd be endangering everyone onboard, including innocent tourists."

"My partners on Moji have organized a fleet of fishing boats. They'll be standing by at Bahia Del Tigre ready to get everyone off the *Dreamseeker* at two-thirty tomorrow afternoon."

O'Malley's face split into a wide grin. "You've even covered that, too?"

Matt nodded. "Now all we have to figure out is how to get Gabriela out of the brig and down here before lockdown. I don't want Scarr taking her hostage when he realizes his ship is going down and he can't escape."

"Timing will be important," said O'Malley. "You can't take her out of the brig too early or Scarr will see that she's missing."

"Any ideas?" Matt asked.

"Now that you mention it, I do. How about a good old-fashioned mutiny?"

* * * * *

It was nearly midnight. Most of the pirates had turned in for the night. Some were in the sleeping quarters and others were in makeshift beds at their workstations. Matt's adrenaline was so high and his brain so wired that he knew he'd never be able to sleep. He sat on the floor of the tiller room chatting to Bart. The large man seemed uncomfortable lying in a hammock that had been strung temporarily from one side of the ship to the tiller head. Matt thought that at any minute the hammock might tip, sending Bart to the floor. How different Bart was from O'Malley. Bart seemed just like everyone else onboard—his hair was unruly and his teeth looked like they had never seen a dentist. It was hard to believe that he was also an agent working undercover.

O'Malley appeared. "It's all set," he whispered, stooping under the low ceiling. "Mutiny on the *Dreamseeker* at 1:30 p.m. tomorrow."

"How have you managed to arranged that?" asked Matt.

"O'Malley and I have been onboard long enough to be trusted by most," said Bart, dropping his pirate accent. "There are quite a few pirates who weren't happy when they heard about Scarr's weapons dealing. They signed up to get the booty and nothing more. There's a big difference between piracy and terrorism. A lot of them are scared they'll get caught. Plus, having Gabriela Kimile locked in the hold has caused quite a stir."

"Skimmy McFinn's really upset," said O'Malley. "For him the last straw was seeing Billy Rogers push your friend Varl down the steps the other day."

Matt got up off the floor and ducked under the swinging hammock to face O'Malley. "What are you saying? Skimmy's going to be part of the mutiny?"

"Yes, but he doesn't know it yet." O'Malley chuckled.

Matt was confused by that answer, but decided O'Malley knew what he was doing. "Did you find some wood to stop the airlock doors from closing?" he asked.

"All ready to go," said O'Malley.

Bart folded his hands behind his head and yawned loudly. "Timing will have to be absolutely perfect, you realize."

"I know," said O'Malley. "And it's a little worrying how close all these events will have to run."

"Then go and get some sleep, the pair of ye!" said Bart, putting on his thick Irish pirate accent. He closed his eyes and said, "It'll be a long day tomorrow. Just maybe tomorrow night I'll be able to sleep in a regular bed for a change!"

Chapter 21

M att looked at his watch. It was nearly time to start the chain of events that would destroy the second Keeper and win him the fifth and final level of his game. He closed his laptop having reread all of the rhymes. He was sure that he'd followed all the clues and there was nothing left to do, so he put it back in his backpack. In spite of all the planning his heart was racing. "That's a good thing," he told himself. He remembered his grandpa telling him that you make fewer mistakes if you're not overconfident.

O'Malley came through the door of the storeroom. "Get any sleep?" he asked.

"Some," said Matt, although really he'd just dozed. "I just want to get this done."

"Well, it's one o'clock, so let's get this started," said O'Malley. "You ready?"

Matt positioned his scarf, shoved a few straggly strands of hair underneath it and then nodded.

"Okay, you look fine. I'll walk you to the steps, just like we've done several times before."

No one questioned Matt or O'Malley as they walked through the hold. Matt was glad he'd taken part in the raid and delivered messages down here so that no one thought anything of his comings and goings.

He followed O'Malley up the steps, through the various rooms on Orlop deck and to the tiller room.

Bart was waiting. He touched Matt lightly on the shoulder. "It'll be fine," he said in a reassuring way. "I've gathered our potential mutineers on the Main deck and they're waiting to hear what O'Malley has to say. Happily, they're already angry about being kept waiting—just the emotions we need to start a good mutiny! From 'ere on in, it's pirate accent."

Bart led the way up to Main deck and toward the assembled group. Matt hung back behind O'Malley. There were at least twenty pirates, all of whom looked unhappy before O'Malley opened his mouth. Skimmy McFinn stood on the edge of the group, his arms wrapped around the main mast. He had a vacant look on his face as if he wasn't quite sure if he wanted to be involved. Matt hoped that O'Malley had read him properly and that Skimmy would take part in whatever O'Malley had planned.

"Me brothers," said O'Malley. "I've not bin 'appy for a long time about the things I see 'appenin' onboard this 'ere ship."

"Aye," shouted Bart from the back. "Me neither. I ain't bin paid from the pickin's for two weeks, and now I 'ear that the booty 'as gone missin'!"

There were mutterings of disbelief from several of the men.

"Nah, you must 'ave it wrong," said one. "Scarr 'as a

special 'idin' place on Moji that no one can get to. Skimmy'll tell ye—'e's seen it!"

Everyone turned to look at Skimmy, whose mouth dropped.

"Well, Skimmy?" said O'Malley. "Tell 'em all what you saw the other night!"

Skimmy shrugged and then said in a whisper, "The booty ain't there no more."

There were shouts of anger and some pushing and shoving. More pirates crowded round the original group until the numbers swelled to around thirty-five.

"Why do ye all think Gabriela Kimile is locked in our brig?" asked O'Malley.

"There's bin rumors," said Bart, pushing forward to the center of the group, "but we ain't bin told by Scarr."

"Cuz it's 'er daddy that's stole all of our booty," said O'Malley. "So now the Cap'n's holding a poor girl 'ostage cuz 'e ain't got the guts to go after 'er old man! Now, is that right, I ask yer?"

The jeering grew loud.

"And that's not the 'alf of it," said O'Malley, having to shout above the din. "Do yer know what Scarr's bin buyin' with our booty? Do yer 'ave any idea what the man, our Cap'n, is *really* doin'? Tell 'em all, Skimmy!"

Everyone else in the group, including Matt, turned to look at Skimmy McFinn. There was sudden silence.

"Well, tell us, Skimmy!" one of the pirates screamed.

Skimmy had turned white. "Cap'n . . . Cap'n . . . Cap'n Scarr," he stammered. "'e's . . . 'e's bin buyin' weapons. Big missile things in 'uge crates. But they've bin stolen along with our booty."

"Buyin' weapons," repeated O'Malley. "Did ye 'ear that? Scarr's bin buyin' weapons with our booty! That money should 'ave bin divided amongst us. But our cap'n ain't bin 'onest about 'ow much our raids 'ave bin fetchin'. I've seen that booty meself! More money than we can carry! An' where is it all? 'ow much of it 'ave we 'ad?"

"We want our money!" demanded Bart, raising his fist in the air. "Who's with me, me mateys? Let's demand our rightful money!"

"And Skimmy, since it's your turn to watch Miss Kimile, you should free 'er," said O'Malley. "We may 'ave bin stealin' from the rich, but since when 'ave we behaved like real pirates where a young lady is concerned?"

There were many shouts of, "Free 'er! Free 'er, Skimmy!"

Matt watched Skimmy skulk to the back of the group. He hesitated on the edge for a moment and then headed down the deck towards the brig. O'Malley nodded at Matt and they both backed to the edge of the group, just as Scarr approached with Hawkeye at his side.

Scarr's face was red with rage. His beady eyes looked as though they were about to shoot from his puffy face. "Silence!" he bellowed. "I will 'ear your grievances after we've done our tour. We're expectin' our visitors to arrive at any moment."

"Now! Now! Now!" the pirates chanted.

"Listen to the Cap'n," said Hawkeye. "We can settle

this after the tour."

"Let's talk about it now!" said Bart. "Our visitors don't get 'ere for another twenty minutes. We've got plenty of time."

"Now! Now! Now!" the pirates chanted.

Scarr and Hawkeye were completely encircled by men, and more were still joining the group.

Matt saw his opportunity. He left the group and walked toward the bow. Skimmy was unlocking the hatch doors to the brig. Perfect! All he had to do was wait for Gabriela to emerge and then whisk her down to the hold. He was sure that Skimmy would do nothing.

Matt watched Gabriela's head appear through the hatch. He was about to rush forward when he noticed Billy Rogers approaching Skimmy. The two men started to argue next to the hatch, Billy occasionally shoving Skimmy.

"Zang it!" Matt whispered to himself. What should he do? He dared not get too close because Billy would recognize him, for sure.

"Come on, Billy!" shouted Skimmy. "It ain't right that the poor girl should be down there."

"I told ye that ye were too soft!" snapped Billy. "'ow do ye think that the Cap'n will get our booty back if 'e don't 'ave 'er for insurance?"

"But it ain't right!" screamed Skimmy. "She ain't nought to do with it all."

Matt's heart raced. If Billy convinced Skimmy to lock the hatch again, he'd have to intervene and risk being recognized. He looked at his watch. Time was running out. He had less than ten minutes until lockdown. He had to start making decisions and taking action.

Suddenly Gabriela's head appeared through the hatch! Then she climbed up a little higher until she was stooped low with her foot on the top step. Gabriela was going to attempt to escape on her own!

"Go for it, Gabriela!" muttered Matt.

Matt moved so he had a plain view of the hatch. Billy had his back to him and he and Skimmy were still arguing.

Gabriela looked around as if trying to decide which direction to run. Matt beckoned her furiously. When she saw him, her eyes widened and she pelted across the deck toward him. He took her hand and pulled her toward the hatch down to Gun deck. Just six minutes to go before lockdown!

"Oy! Where's the girl gone?" shouted Billy.

Matt shoved Gabriela down the hatch.

"The girl's escaped!" shouted Billy. "Find 'er!"

Matt quickly slipped out of sight. Would anyone even hear Billy with all the ruckus?

"This way," said Matt to Gabriela.

The warning siren sounded. Five minutes.

Gabriela looked alarmed.

"Don't worry," said Matt. "It's nothing to do with you escaping."

They ran straight down the center of Gun deck, climbed backwards down the ladder into the tiller room, and ran through the surgeon's cockpit into the powder room.

The hatch opened. Someone was coming up! Matt quickly pushed Gabriela between the stacked barrels then stood in front to conceal her. Two men came up from below, dressed in pirate gear ready for the tour.

"Ye should 'urry up on deck," said Matt. "Cap'n Scarr, 'e be talking to everyone."

"Thanks," the men muttered.

Matt smiled at them and waited a few seconds. Now could he get Gabriela down the steps? Three minutes to go. The hatch opened again. Oh no! Not another person!

"What's goin' on?" asked another pirate, poking his head through the hatch.

"Cap'n's talkin' to everyone on Main deck. Best ye 'urry."

The man scurried up the steps.

"Ye the last?" asked Matt.

"Think so," replied the pirate, hurrying away.

Matt felt sick. Where was O'Malley? If he was still on deck there was nothing Matt could do about it.

He waited for the men to disappear from view and then threw open the hatch. "Down there, quick!" he ordered Gabriela.

She flew across the room and through the hatch. Matt climbed down backwards after her. He was about to reach up to close the hatch when the second siren sounded and it sprang closed on its own, slamming loudly above his head and almost catching his fingers.

Matt's feet touched the floor and he sighed with relief. He felt a hand on his shoulder and sprang around, heart racing again.

It was O'Malley. "That was cutting it close!" he said, a look of complete relief on his face.

"I know," said Matt. "And I thought *you* hadn't made it back down here!"

Gabriela stood in silence, shaking. She looked at both of them with fear in her eyes.

"It's okay," said Matt. "I'm Matt and this is O'Malley. We're Targon's friends. You're safe with us."

"Targon's friends?" she questioned. "How did he know I'd been kidnapped? How did he tell you? How did you get onboard?"

"Long story," said Matt. "We'll explain later. No one can get down here for now, but we have to work fast to get you out of here."

"We'll be ready to go in about ten minutes," said O'Malley. "Just sit here on the floor, Gabriela, and wait for us, okay?"

She nodded.

Matt followed O'Malley across the hold to the lockers. "We may have a problem," he whispered. "Billy Rogers caused some last-minute trouble. He saw me running away with Gabriela."

"Let's hope that Scarr is too preoccupied with the mutineers and the tourists coming aboard to think about the hold. He saw me up on deck a minute ago, so let's hope he won't realize that not everyone was out of the hold when I went up there."

"We'd better work fast, just in case," said Matt.

"First, let's get rid of these clothes," said O'Malley, pulling off his pirate garb.

Matt pulled his tourist clothing and his backpack out of O'Malley's locker. He cringed at the sight of the white shorts and flowery shirt, but they were better than the pirate outfit.

"Ready?" asked O'Malley. He pulled three large blocks of wood, a tape measure and some cloth tape out of his locker.

"Tape?" said Matt in disbelief. "You're going to fasten the wood to the inner airlock door with tape?"

"Inner is the magic word," said O'Malley. "No water will touch the tape until we open the outer doors, and by then it won't matter. The pressure of the other door will hold the blocks in place."

Matt shook his head. "So simple," he said. "All this high-tech machinery around us and we're using wood and tape?"

O'Malley laughed. "Sometimes the good old-fashioned ways are the best," he said, jogging across to the platform that surrounded the airlock. He stepped up and looked down at the mini-subs. "I'll need you to hold the wood blocks in place while I tape them onto the metal door," he said.

Matt turned to look at Gabriela, sat at the bottom of the steps. "Are you okay?" he asked as he stepped up next to O'Malley.

"I'm doing fine now, thanks," she said, forcing a smile.

"The airlock doors are under this platform, but we can just see the edge of each door jutting out," said O'Malley. Matt helped him measure the distance between the sensors on the left door, and in just a couple of minutes they fastened three large blocks of wood opposite the sensors.

"Do we need to disable the other mini-sub?" Matt asked.

"No," O'Malley replied. "By the time that Scarr works out what has happened and overrides the lockdown, the hold will be too flooded for anyone to get to it."

Matt looked at his watch. "The fleet of fishing boats will be in position in fifteen minutes," he said.

"Okay, let's go!" shouted O'Malley. "Gabriela, get up here!"

Gabriela jumped to her feet and ran up to the platform. "We're going where, exactly?" she asked.

"Down here," said O'Malley, climbing through the hatch of the mini-sub.

"You've got to be joking!" she said. "You want *me* in that thing?"

"It's okay, really," said Matt. "I've been in it once and O'Malley knows what he's doing. You want to get off this ship, don't you?"

"Of course," she said. She gritted her teeth and climbed through the hatch.

Matt took a quick look around the hold. He felt almost

sad that he was sending all of this valuable computer equipment to the bottom of the ocean, but it was the only way to complete Level 5 of his game and put Scarr out of action permanently.

O'Malley locked the hatch and took his seat at the controls.

"Can't you leave the hatch open until you've closed the inner airlock doors?" Matt asked. "Then we can check that the blocks of wood are holding."

"Sorry," said O'Malley. "There's only a couple of inches' clearance. Got to close the hatch first."

"I guess we won't know if it worked until we reach the surface," said Matt.

"Buckle up, both of you," said O'Malley. "Okay, closing inner doors now."

Matt nervously held his breath. He could see the windows behind him darken as the doors were moved into position. Would their plan work?

"The controls are showing the doors have closed," said O'Malley. "So hopefully our blocks of wood are in place. I'm going to open the outer doors now."

Matt let out his breath. He heard the engines fire up, and then grating metal, then finally rushing water. The mini-sub seemed to need more power than before to leave the airlock. Was that a good sign?

Chapter 22

M att felt a jolt as the mini-sub surfaced. He looked at his watch. It was 2:35 p.m. Had Varl and Targon succeeded in organizing enough fishing boats to take everyone off the *Dreamseeker*? The seawater lapped against the portholes making it impossible for him to see through the windows. His heart raced as O'Malley opened the hatch.

Matt climbed up the steps and stuck his head into the fresh air. The *Dreamseeker* was low in the water and a flotilla of small fishing boats was lined up to take passengers off. He felt euphoric. Before long the *Dreamseeker* would disappear below the surface.

"The blocks of wood obviously held," said O'Malley, looking through his turret window.

"We've done a great job," said Matt, ducking his head back inside for a moment. "She's definitely sinking, and the boats are already taking off the tourists."

"I don't know quite what this has all been about," said Gabriela, "but thanks for getting me off the ship and away from Scarr. Although I'm not sure how I'm going to feel about going back to Pueblo Verde. Everyone will hate me."

"No they won't," said O'Malley. "You're not responsible for what your father has done. There are plenty of people who will be very pleased to see you."

"Targon, for one," said Matt. "He was so worried about you. And I expect that Jarro will have contacted your mother by now."

"I can't wait to see her," said Gabriela, blinking back the tears.

Matt stuck his head back into the fresh air. "Can you maneuver the sub around? I can't see the police cruiser."

"Sure," said O'Malley.

They turned towards the *Dreamseeker's* stern.

"Scarr's in the jolly boat!" yelled Matt. "And I think that's Hawkeye with him. They're making a run for it!"

"Close the hatch! I'll cut him off!" said O'Malley.

"Can you radio for help?" asked Matt.

O'Malley put on the headphones and fiddled with the radio frequency.

"He's not going to get far in a row boat," said Gabriela.

"If he reaches the island he may have contacts that can hide him. He could easily disappear," said O'Malley. "Hold on, everyone!" He revved the engines and took the mini-sub across the surface at speed, talking on the radio as he navigated.

"Wow! This thing is amazing," said Matt. "It's a cross between a submarine and a speed boat."

Suddenly O'Malley cut the engines. He grabbed an EPE from under his seat and leaped up the steps and through the hatch.

"Scarr, don't move or I'll shoot!" bellowed O'Malley.

Matt came through the hatch to see O'Malley straddled on the flat top of the mini-sub, his EPE pointed at Persivius Scarr and Hawkeye. Both pirates looked like comic book characters sat in the rowboat with their hands above their heads and innocent, almost silly grins on their faces.

Scarr saw Matt and his face darkened instantly. "You, boy?" he said with venom. "I don't know what you've got to do with all this, but me problems started when you came aboard me ship!"

"You can cut the fake pirate accent," said Matt. "You won't be needing it where you're going."

A police cruiser pulled up alongside, and two police officers jumped aboard and handcuffed Scarr and Hawkeye. Someone shouted from the back of the police cruiser. Matt turned to see Varl and Targon excitedly waving at him.

"Well done, my boy!" said Varl.

"Matt! Did you find Gabriela?" shouted Targon.

Matt ducked inside the mini-sub. "I think you'd better show yourself," he said, virtually pushing Gabriela up top.

"Okay," said O'Malley, "let's head for the shore and you can talk to your friends some more. I think it's about time I met this incredible team of undercover agents."

"Undercover agents?" said Gabriela.

Matt smiled. He was tired of making up stories. "I'm sure that Targon will tell you all about it," he said.

* * * * *

Matt sat on the pier at Bahia Del Tigre with his computer open on his lap, his feet dangling inches above the water. He looked out to sea at the setting sun, finally able to relax enough to enjoy the beautiful reds and pinks of the evening sky. Varl and Targon sat on either side of him.

"You looked so different with black hair," said Targon. "I hardly recognized you."

"I was glad to have a shower and get most of the dye out," said Matt. "Though it took several tries."

"I'm just glad we escaped the festivities," said Varl. "I've done enough celebrating to last me the rest of my life."

"O'Malley and Jarro will be heroes forever," said Matt.

"I think it all turned out okay," said Targon. "I'm sad for Gabriela, but her mother seemed really nice. At least we saved more cruise ships from being attacked by pirates, and helped the people on this island keep the tourists and their jobs."

"I think we did a lot more than that!" said Matt. "The safety of the entire world, and not just a kingdom or an empire was at risk this time. Scarr could have held so many governments to ransom with his CGP's."

"Quite true, my boy," said Varl. "And it's a fitting end to your *Keeper of the Kingdom* game that the CGP's will all be destroyed and Scarr will be held accountable for his actions. So finally, why don't you get us all home!"

"I'm ready," said Matt. "Enough is enough. I don't think I'll be playing another computer game for a *long* time."

"Well, go on then—enter the final commands," said Varl. "And make sure you press the right keys!"

Matt smiled. He read out loud, "Congratulations! You have completed the final level successfully and finished the game, *Keeper of the Kingdom.*"

"Well, that seems final enough this time," said Varl.

Matt looked up at him and his stomach tightened. For a moment he wondered if he really wanted to go home. "It's been nice working with you, Varl. It's going to seem strange without you. I hope that you and Targon both have a safe trip back to Zaul."

"And you too, my boy." Varl patted him on the back. "I'm going to miss you."

"Take care, Matt from 2010," said Targon with a long face. "I've enjoyed our adventures. It's been a lot of fun."

"Yes, it has," said Matt. He reached around for the helmet that he'd worn on the raid. "O'Malley said I can keep this as a souvenir." He put it on to show them. "Pity I didn't keep anything else from my travels."

"You'll have memories enough," said Varl.

"Well, I guess I'll press '*Exit*' one last time," said Matt, looking through the acrylic visor at his keyboard.

He held his breath as he pressed the key. A small box containing a purple X appeared. He clicked on the X to end his game. Purple words materialized on the screen.

Continue to evaluation. High scorer will be revealed.

Then everything went black.

Matt suddenly found himself floundering in the dark. He couldn't see! Sheer fright swept through him. His hands hit cushioned walls. He gasped for air, panting in terror. What was happening? Where was he?

An important note from H.J. Ralles

For those of you who've read Matt's name
In every book throughout his game
It is the time to see how fast
You've learned the lessons of the past
Now you are about to find
The ending that I had in mind
See, you are completely hooked
You have to finish one more book
But I am hoping you have come
To learn that reading's lots of fun
Instead of pictures on a screen
My words will make my story seen
Turning the page is just the same
As playing levels in your game
I'm the author—that's my domain
Which means I'm the Keeper of Matt's game!

Read the final scenario if you dare!

Epilogue

Matt's heart raced. He couldn't breathe. It was pitch black and someone's hands were around his neck! He tried to push them away. His right arm hit a wall. Where was he? It seemed as though he was in some kind of enclosure.

Then he heard a deep voice. "Matt! It's okay. I'm only undoing your helmet! Don't fight me!"

Was that O'Malley talking to him? Was he back in the mini-sub? Had Level 5 not finished after all?

"Matt! Can you hear me? Take off your helmet! You're done."

Someone pulled him forward and yanked off his helmet.

The bright light blinded him. He rubbed his eyes and saw that he was in a large room, surrounded by computers and high-definition screens. A middle-aged man with a receding hairline and droopy moustache stood before him holding a black helmet with an acrylic visor.

"Where am I?" Matt asked. "Is that my souvenir from Moji?"

"Jeez, you really did get involved in the game," the man replied. "It's over, Matt. It's all over. You won!"

"Won?"

"You got 96%—the highest score to date!"

"I did?"

"You don't even know who I am, do you?"

Matt shook his head.

"I'm David Greer and you're at Virtual Game Development Corporation. I'm the manager in charge of new product testing. You agreed to evaluate our new *Keeper of the Kingdom* game, remember?"

It was as if he'd been pulled out of the darkness. "Oh! That's right!" said Matt. "Now I remember coming here."

"Let's see how your fellow gamers are doing, shall we?"

"Fellow gamers?" questioned Matt.

David Greer turned him around to face a row of large coffin-shaped pods, one of which was open.

Matt shivered. "What are they?"

"They're the gaming booths. You've just come out of booth #1."

Matt stared at the open booth. He had a vague recollection of getting into it, but it seemed a distant memory. In fact it felt like years ago. It had padded velvet walls, a built-in seat, and two sets of surround-sound speakers. A personal computer was on a stand attached to the open door.

David Greer opened up booth #2. "You're done, young man. Game over," he said, helping him out.

The blond boy rubbed his eyes. "Wow! That was some wild ride! Hey! You're Matt, right?"

"Targon?" Matt gasped, trying to take it all in.

"Actually my name's *really* Tony Argon—but before I started the game, Mr. Greer told me I had to use a single screen name."

"Tony, eh?" said Matt. "That'll take some getting used to."

"No problem—I'm cool with Targon. So, how did you do, bud? Did I beat you?"

David Greer shook his head. "Sorry, Tony. You came close—90%. It's a good score—but not good enough to beat Matt."

Targon groaned. "Zang it! I felt sure I'd won."

David Greer opened booth #3 and helped out a third gamer. "You remember Robert Varl, our chief game designer, don't you?"

Matt nearly collapsed with the shock. "It's Varl!" he said.

"Hello, Matt, my boy. Glad you liked my new virtual experience. Had to try it out myself to make sure there weren't any problems."

"So that's why you were such a technical whiz!" laughed Matt.

"It seems the game was too easy for you," said Varl.

"I wouldn't say that," said Matt. "It took some doing."

Varl placed his arm around Matt's shoulders. "Perhaps I should make it more difficult. Virtual Game Development Corporation won't make any money if everyone gets through all five levels on the first attempt!"

"But they won't all have you helping them, Robert,"

said David Greer. "You did have inside knowledge when it counted, and I'm sure that you must have given away a few secrets."

"Give the boy some credit!" said Varl. "I gave away very little. But Matt, I'll need you to sit down with me and talk about improvements."

"And me, too?" asked Targon.

"But of course," said Varl.

"Oh! We're forgetting someone," said David Greer, walking over to booth #4 and unlatching it.

Matt drew breath as the booth opened. Who would it be this time? Out bounced a vibrant girl with thick wavy ginger hair and gold hoop earrings. "Angel!" he screamed. "What are *you* doing here?"

"Having fun," she said, tossing back her hair. "You look like that Matt kid in the game."

"I am. I'm Matt Hammond."

"And I'm Targon—Tony Argon."

"Yeah, I recognize you too," she said.

"But we left you in the Empire of Gova!" said Matt. "Level 3, *Keeper of the Empire*, right?"

"Angel was also Dana in Level 1, Keela in Level 2, Bronya in Level 4 and Gabriela in this final level of your game—with a little help from computer graphics, of course," said David Greer. "It's wonderful being able to play around with everything from facial features to clothing and even accents—a new girl in every level!"

"Actually, my real name is Angelica Varl, but Grandpa has always called me Angel." She turned to Varl and said, "So, how did I do, Grandpa?"

"Grandpa?" said Matt and Targon in unison. "Varl's your grandfather?"

Angel grinned. "Yeah, he's pretty cool for a grandfather, isn't he?"

Varl hugged her. "Thanks, Angel!"

"So, did I beat them both?" she asked him.

"You did just great—92%," said Varl. "A good percentile. *And* you beat Targon—but you didn't get the high score, sorry."

"But I will next time," she said, looking at Matt.

"Next time?" said Matt. "Aren't we done?"

"*Keeper of the Kingdom* will be out in the stores in four months—just in time for the holidays," said David Greer. "But Robert has been working on a new game for next year."

"You'll love it, Matt, my boy," Varl said. "You'll be fixated— just you wait and see! The villains are even more creative and the tasks even harder. My new game will have you beat, for sure."

Matt raised his eyebrows. "I think I'll need a year to recover from this one first."

Robert Varl laughed. "I'll take that as a compliment. I'm certainly going to have plenty more games for you to test over the next few years. Did you know that by 2015 over 50% of families in the U.S.A. will have a virtual gaming booth in their homes?"

"Which is great news for Virtual Game Development Corporation," said David Greer. He lifted Matt's denim jacket off a coat hook by the door and threw it to him. "Go home and get some rest," he said. "We'll see you *all* back here on Monday for an evaluation of *Keeper of the Kingdom*. Thank you for giving up your time to test our product. You can pick up your checks on Monday after you complete the evaluation."

Matt walked out of the room, through the plush lobby and the revolving doors beyond. He stood under the portico for a second and breathed in deeply. The fresh air smelled so good. For a moment he felt disorientated. "Where do I go now?" He stared at the sub shop on the corner, the post office next to it and the heavy traffic that zoomed past. "Oh yeah, the bus stop's across the road," he muttered.

Targon came up behind him. "Weird, isn't it?"

"Yeah. It's like I've been away on some long vacation."

"Zaul was no vacation!"

Matt laughed. "Yeah, vacation isn't the right word."

"Well, I'll see ya," said Targon, setting off down the street.

"Yeah—Monday morning."

Matt stepped into the sunshine, and as he walked across the street to the bus stop, he couldn't help but remember the chilling laboratories in Zaul and the icy colony of Javeer. Boy, was he ever glad to feel the warmth of the sun on his face!

He sat down on the wooden bench to wait for the bus and looked at the people passing by. For a moment he thought he saw Conan O'Malley in the crowd—and was that Hawkeye across the street? Was Scarr here too? He got to his feet, his heart pounding.

"It's difficult to switch off, isn't it?" said Angel.

The sound of her voice shook him back to reality. Matt turned and stared at her broad grin and bouncing ginger curls and he relaxed. He felt as though his teacher had just told him that he didn't have to retake the math test. "Yeah. It's like my brain is still telling me to look out for Vorgs and run from Captain Scarr."

Angel laughed. "I *really* thought I was in all of those places. I'm sure I'll have nightmares for weeks!"

"Your grandfather did a good job with that game," said Matt.

"It'll be a bestseller, for sure." She pulled out a pack of gum. "Want some?"

Matt eagerly took a piece. "Spearmint. There's a flavor I've missed! It sure beats lingoones and Bee's stew."

Angel giggled. "Missed? We've only been here a few hours, Matt Hammond!"

"Still, it's been a *long* day."

"And you didn't eat any of that stuff for real, you know!"

"Yeah, I know—but I feel as though I can taste them all! And now I crave pizza and Mom's brownies."

"Well, here's my bus. I guess I'll see you on Monday."

"Sure." Matt waved her goodbye and sat back down on the bench to wait for his own bus. A sudden wave of happiness passed over him when he realized that he hadn't left his friends behind after all. And was he ever glad it was 2010 and not 2540! Perhaps he could persuade his brother Jake to come with him next time he tested a game. After all, it was a great way to earn money during the summer vacation.

"Next time?" he said out loud. What *was* he thinking?

About the Author

H.J. Ralles lives in a Dallas suburb with her husband, two teenage sons and a devoted black Labrador. *Keeper of the Island* is her seventh novel.

Visit H.J. Ralles at her website www.hjralles.com

Also by H.J. Ralles

The Keeper Series

Keeper of the Kingdom

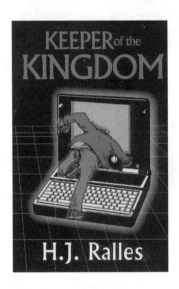

Book I
ISBN 1-929976-03-8 Top Publications

In 2540AD, the Kingdom of Zaul is an inhospitable world controlled by Cybergon 'Protectors' and ruled by 'The Keeper'. Humans are 'Worker' slaves, eliminated without thought. Thank goodness this is just a computer game – or is it? For Matt, the Kingdom of Zaul becomes all too real when his computer jams and he is sucked into the game. Now he is trapped, hunted by the Protectors and hiding among the Workers to survive. Matt must use his knowledge of computers and technology to free the people of Zaul and return to his own world. *Keeper of the Kingdom* is a gripping tale of technology out of control.

Keeper of the Realm

Book II
ISBN 1-929976-21-6 Top Publications, Ltd.

In 2540 AD, the peaceful realm of Karn, 300 feet below sea level, has been invaded by the evil Noxerans. This beautiful city has become a prison for the Karns who must obey Noxeran regulations or die at their hands. In the second thrilling adventure of the Keeper Series, Matt uncovers the secrets of the underwater world. He must rid the realm of the Noxerans and destroy the Keeper. But winning Level two of his game, without obliterating Karn, looks to be an impossible task. Can Matt find the Keeper before it's too late for them all?

Keeper of the Empire

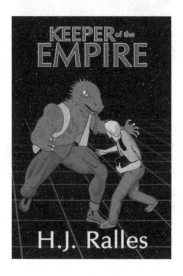

Book III

ISBN 1-929976-25-9 Top Publications, Ltd.

The Vorgs have landed! They're grotesque, they spit venom and Matt is about to be their next victim. What are these lizard-like creatures doing in Gova? Why are humans wandering around like zombies? In the third book of the Keeper series, Matt finds himself in a terrifying world. With the help of his friend Targon, and a daring girl named Angel, Matt must locate the secret hideout of the Govan Resistance. And what has become of the wise old scientist, Varl? There is no end to the action and excitement as Matt attempts to track down the Keeper, and win the next level of his computer game.

Keeper of the Colony

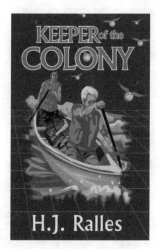

Book IV

ISBN # 1-929976-35-6   Top Publications   March 2006

Beware! When the curfew bell tolls in the Dark End you had better be off the street! The icy Colony of Javeer, brutally ruled by Horando and his Gulden Guard, is a horrific setting for Level 4 of Matt's computer game. Targon has disappeared and Varl has been arrested and thrown into Central Jail. When Matt attempts to rescue Varl with the help of his new friends, Keir and Bronya Logan, he learns that Horando is not the only enemy he must beat. Gnashers live deep in the gold mines and are killing humans that dare to enter. But Horando will stop at nothing when it comes to increasing his stock of gold—even if it means sending thousands of humans to their death. Can Matt defeat Horando and save Varl before he becomes the next victim of the Gnashers?

The Darok Series

Darok 9

Book I
ISBN 1-929976-10-0 Top Publications, Ltd.

In 2120 AD, the barren surface of the moon is the only home that three generations of Earth's survivors have ever known. Towns, called Daroks, protect inhabitants from the extreme lunar temperatures. But life is harsh. Hank Havard, a young scientist, is secretly perfecting SH33, a drug that eliminates the body's need for water. When his First Quadrant laboratory is attacked, Hank saves his research onto a memory card and runs from the enemy. Aided by Will, his teenaged nephew, and Maddie, Will's computer-wizard classmate, Hank must conceal SH33 from the dreaded Fourth Quadrant. But suddenly Will's life is in danger. Who can Hank trust- and is the enemy really closer to home?

Darok 10

Book II
ISBN 1-929976-31-3 Top Publications, Ltd.

Dr. Gunter Schumann has mysteriously vanished from the lunar colony, Darok 9. Was he kidnapped? And what is the significance of the sinister discovery by scientist Hank Havard and Will, his fourteen-year-old nephew? Determined to solve the mystery, Will and his friend Maddie travel to neighboring Darok 10 in search of the truth. But when Will is captured by a ruthless killer bent on destroying the Daroks, Maddie and Hank are forced to steal military secrets. Can they prevent a lunar war and the destruction of humankind?